Granny's Ghost and the Movie Night Murder

Ghostly Gumshoe Cozy Mysteries Series, Volume 5

Sloane Finley

Published by Ginger and Spice Publishing, 2025.

GRANNY'S GHOST AND THE MOVIE NIGHT MURDER

First edition. July 11, 2025.

ISBN: 979-8231752300

Written by Sloane Finley.

Table of Contents

Chapter 1

The shrill ring of my phone cuts through the peaceful quiet of my Victorian home. I'm elbow-deep in sudsy water, washing the breakfast dishes, when Charlie's name flashes across the screen. With a sigh, I dry my hands on a nearby towel and answer.

"Lena! Oh my god, you're never going to believe this!" her voice bursts through the speaker.

I can't help but smile at my best friend's enthusiasm. "Slow down, Charlie. What's got you so worked up this early in the morning?"

"Marianne Olsen is coming back to New Oslo!"

The name hits me like a punch to the gut. Marianne Olsen. I haven't heard that name in years, not since she left our little town in the dust to pursue her Hollywood dreams. Memories of high school flood back—the whispered insults, the stolen lunch money, the complicated web of social hierarchies that seemed so important back then.

"What do you mean, she's coming back?" I ask, trying to sound nonchalant.

Charlie's words tumble out in a rush. "She's got a new movie coming out—some made-for-TV horror flick. Apparently, she's decided to host her own viewing party here in New Oslo. Can you believe it? Our very own Hollywood star, coming back to grace us with her presence!"

I can hear the mix of excitement and sarcasm in Charlie's voice. She and I were never exactly friends with Marianne in high school. In fact, we were often on the receiving end of her mean girl antics. But now, even Charlie seems a little star-struck by the idea of Marianne's return.

"When is this happening?" I ask, already dreading the answer.

"Next week!" Charlie exclaims. "The whole town's going to be in an uproar. You know how people get when there's even a whiff of celebrity around here."

I do know. New Oslo isn't exactly a hotbed of excitement most days. The return of Marianne Olsen, now a bona fide TV star, is bound to set tongues wagging and tempers flaring.

"Look," Charlie continues, her voice taking on a conspiratorial tone, "I know you and Marianne had your... issues in high school. But this could be huge for the town. We should do something to welcome her back, don't you think? Maybe it's time to bury the hatchet."

I hesitate, memories of my last interaction with Marianne flashing through my mind. The harsh words, the tears, the promises to "never amount to anything." But that was years ago. We were just kids then, weren't we?

"I don't know, Charlie," I say slowly. "It's been a long time. Maybe it's best to just let her do her thing and leave the past in the past."

Charlie scoffs. "Come on, Lena! Where's your sense of adventure? This could be fun! Plus, what better way to prove that you're the bigger person who has moved on and let bygones be bygones?"

Charlie has always been the one to push me out of my comfort zone, and more often than not, I'm grateful for it. Even if it does sometimes lead to trouble.

"Okay, okay," I concede. "What did you have in mind?"

As Charlie launches into her ideas, I find myself swept up in her excitement. Maybe this won't be so bad after all. Maybe Marianne has changed. Maybe we all have.

We agree to meet at Betty's Diner to discuss further, and I hang up the phone with a mix of anticipation and dread swirling in my stomach.

A little while later, that sense of dread and anticipation is still as strong as ever as I push open the door to the diner. It's mid-morning, and the familiar scent of coffee and fresh-baked pie washes over me like a delicious wave. The place is bustling with the usual crowd of regulars, their chatter filling the air.

I slide into a nearby booth, nodding a greeting to Betty as she bustles past with a pot of coffee. She returns a moment later, filling my mug without asking. That's one of the things I love about small towns – everyone knows your habits.

"Have you heard the news?" Betty asks, her eyes twinkling with excitement. "About Marianne Olsen?"

I nod, wrapping my hands around the warm mug. "Charlie filled me in this morning. Quite the surprise, isn't it?"

Betty leans in, lowering her voice conspiratorially. "You're telling me! Who would have thought our little Marianne would make it big in Hollywood? And now she's coming back for a movie premiere, of all things!"

As Betty moves on to her next customer, I can't help but overhear the conversations buzzing around me. It seems Marianne's return is the talk of the town.

"...always knew she'd make it big," I hear Mrs. Johnson saying at the counter. "That girl had star quality from the day she was born. Remember her in the school play? Stole the show, she did!"

But not everyone seems as enthusiastic. From the booth behind me, I catch snippets of a less flattering conversation.

"...thinks she's too good for us now," grumbles my science teacher, Mr. Moore. "Bet she's just coming back to show off, rub our noses in her fancy Hollywood life."

I sink lower in my seat, trying to blend into the vinyl upholstery. It's strange, hearing people talk about Marianne like this. In my mind, she's still the girl I knew in high school—beautiful, ambitious, and yes, sometimes cruel. But a star? It's hard to reconcile that image with the Marianne I remember.

Charlie arrives, sliding into the seat across from me with a grin that immediately sets me on edge. I know that look. It's the look she gets when she's about to suggest something outrageous.

"So," she says, leaning forward conspiratorially, "I've been thinking about what we can do to bury the hatchet with Marianne."

I groan inwardly. "Charlie, please tell me you haven't done anything yet."

Her grin widens. "Not yet. But I've got an idea. A brilliant idea, if I do say so myself."

I brace myself. "Alright, let's hear it."

"We should hold the viewing party at your house!" she exclaims, thankfully keeping her voice low enough that the other patrons don't turn to stare. "It's perfect! That big Victorian of yours is exactly what we need. It's spacious, it's got that historic charm, and it's neutral territory. No one can accuse anyone of playing favorites if it's held at a private residence."

I blink, taken aback. "My house? Charlie, are you serious? That's... that's crazy!"

But even as I protest, I can see the logic in her suggestion. My house is one of the largest private residences in New Oslo, a sprawling Victorian that's been in my family for generations. It's got a formal parlor that could easily accommodate a small crowd, and the wraparound porch would be perfect for mingling. Plus, it's right there on Main Street.

I chew my lip, considering. "I don't know, Charlie. It's a lot to take on. And what about Marianne? What if she doesn't want to come to my house?"

Charlie's expression softens. "Lena, that's ancient history. She probably doesn't even remember all that mean stuff she did to us back then. I'm sure Marianne has grown up, just like we have. Besides, it's not like she can really refuse if half the town has already said they'll show up."

"Half the town?" I'm starting to feel lightheaded. "Please tell me you haven't actually invited that many people already."

"Well, not yet." Charlie looks a little sheepish, and I wonder if she's telling me the whole truth. "But I'm sure there will be tons of people who want to be a part of something like this."

I look around the diner, my mind whirling. The place has seen its fair share of town events over the years. But a Hollywood premiere? That's a whole different ballgame.

"It would be a lot of work," I muse aloud. "The house would need a deep clean, we'd have to rearrange furniture, sort out catering..."

Charlie's grin widens. "So you'll do it?"

I hold up a hand. "I didn't say that. I'm just... considering the logistics."

But even as I say it, I can feel myself being swayed by the idea. There's something exciting about the prospect of hosting such a big event. And Charlie's right—it would be a nice public gesture to show there's no hard feelings between Mariane.

"Look," Charlie says, her voice taking on a gentler tone. "I know it's a lot to ask. But this could be good for you, Lena. Good for the town, too. And who knows? Maybe it's exactly what you need to finally put the past behind you."

I take a deep breath, looking out the diner window at the quiet street of New Oslo. It's a sleepy town most days, but I can already imagine the buzz of excitement that would come with a Hollywood premiere. The lights, the cameras, the glamour...

"Okay," I hear myself say, almost surprised by my own decision. "Okay, I'll do it. But you're helping me with everything, Charlie. I mean it. I'm not taking this on alone."

Charlie lets out a squeal of delight, earning us a few curious glances from nearby tables. "You won't regret this, Lena! It's going to be amazing. Just you wait and see!"

As we start to plan, I can't help but feel more than a little trepidation. Hosting the viewing party is a big step, one that will put me squarely in the spotlight alongside Marianne. I just hope I'm ready for whatever comes next.

After finishing our coffee and hammering out some initial plans, Charlie and I part ways. I decide to swing by the grocery store to pick up a few things, my mind still swirling with thoughts of the upcoming event.

I'm in the produce section, absently squeezing avocados, when a familiar voice makes me freeze.

"Well, well. If it isn't Lena Larson."

I turn slowly, coming face to face with James Peterson. He's leaning casually against a display of apples, a smirk playing at the corners of his mouth. My stomach does an uncomfortable flip.

"Hello, James," I say, trying to keep my voice neutral. "How are you?"

His smirk widens. "Oh, I'm just peachy. Heard the big news about Marianne Olsen coming back to town. Must be exciting for you, huh? Reliving those glory days of high school?"

There's an edge to his voice that makes me uneasy. James and I have a... complicated history. His father, my grandmother's friend and neighbor Herold Peterson, was found dead under mysterious circumstances a while back. I was tangentially involved in the investigation, and while James was never openly hostile, there's always been an undercurrent of tension between us since then.

It doesn't help that he's moved back in to live with his widowed mother... right next door to me.

"It's certainly unexpected," I reply carefully. "But I'm sure it'll be good for the town."

James pushes off from the apple display, taking a step closer. "Yeah, I'm sure it will be. Funny how things come full circle, isn't it? People leaving, people coming back... secrets coming to light."

I feel a chill run down my spine at his words. "What do you mean by that, James?"

He shrugs, his face a mask of innocence. "Oh, nothing specific. Just thinking out loud. You know how it is in small towns—everyone's got their secrets."

Before I can respond, he reaches past me to grab an apple. "Well, I'd better get going. See you around, Lena. I'm sure we'll be running into each other a lot more with all the excitement coming up."

I watch him walk away, my heart pounding. There was something in his tone, in the way he looked at me, that left me feeling unsettled. It's as if he knows something—or thinks he knows something—that I don't.

Shaking off the encounter, I finish my shopping and head home. As I'm putting away the groceries, a familiar chill sweeps through the kitchen. I don't need to turn around to know that Granny's ghost has materialized.

"Lena, dear," her spectral voice calls out. "We need to talk."

I sigh, turning to face the translucent form of my grandmother. She's wearing the same floral dress she always favored in life, her silver hair pulled back in its usual bun. Even as a ghost, she has an air of no-nonsense authority about her.

"Is this about Marianne coming back to town?" I ask, already knowing the answer.

Granny nods, her expression grave. "I don't like it, Lena. That girl always brought trouble with her, even when you were kids. And now, with her coming back... I've got a bad feeling about all this."

I lean against the counter, crossing my arms. "Granny, that was years ago. We've all grown up since then. And besides, it's just a viewing party for her movie. What could possibly go wrong?"

The moment the words leave my mouth, I regret them. In my experience, asking what could go wrong is a surefire way to find out.

Granny's form flickers slightly, a sign of her agitation. "Mark my words, child. There's more to this than meets the eye. You need to be careful. Very careful."

I nod, trying to reassure her (and myself). "I will be, Granny. I promise."

As her form fades away, I'm left alone in the kitchen, the weight of her warning settling over me like a heavy blanket. Between James's cryptic comments and Granny's concern, what should have been an exciting event now feels fraught with unseen dangers.

Chapter 2

The next morning, I wake to the sound of my phone buzzing incessantly. Groaning, I reach for it, squinting at the screen in the early morning light. It's Charlie, of course. Who else would be calling at the crack of dawn?

"Hello?" I mumble, still half-asleep.

"Lena! Get up, sleepyhead. We've got work to do!" Charlie's voice is far too chipper for this hour.

I sit up, rubbing my eyes. "Charlie, it's not even seven o'clock yet. What could possibly be so urgent?"

"The viewing party, of course! We need to start planning. I've already made a list of everything we need to do. Can you meet me at the diner in an hour?"

I sigh, knowing resistance is futile when Charlie gets like this. "Fine, fine. I'll be there."

An hour later, I'm sliding into our usual booth at Betty's Diner, a steaming mug of coffee already waiting for me. Charlie sits across from me, a notebook open in front of her, scribbling furiously.

"Okay," she says without preamble, "I've divided the tasks into categories. Decorations, food, seating arrangements, entertainment..."

I hold up a hand, cutting her off. "Whoa, slow down. Don't you think we should check with Marianne first? Make sure she actually wants to have the viewing party at my house?"

Charlie waves dismissively. "Already taken care of. I reached out to her agent this morning. They love the idea. Apparently,

Marianne's thrilled at the thought of a 'quaint, small-town premiere' in a 'charming historic home.' Her words, not mine."

I blink, surprised. "Oh. Well, I guess that's... good?"

"It's more than good, it's perfect!" Charlie beams. "Now, let's talk logistics. We'll need to rearrange your living room to accommodate the screen and seating. Oh, and we should probably do something about that creaky floorboard by the fireplace..."

As Charlie rattles on, I find my mind wandering. I picture Marianne walking into my house, that familiar smirk on her face. Will she make some snide comment about the decor? Or worse, will she pretend that everything's fine between us, ignoring our troubled history?

"Lena? Are you even listening to me?" Charlie's voice snaps me back to reality.

"Sorry, I was just... thinking."

Charlie's expression softens. "Having second thoughts?"

I shake my head. "No, not exactly. It's just... strange, you know? Marianne coming back after all this time. Us hosting her premiere. It feels a bit like we're back in high school, trying to impress the popular girl."

"Hey," Charlie reaches across the table, squeezing my hand. "We're not those insecure teenagers anymore. We're doing this on our terms. And if Marianne can't appreciate that, well, that's her problem."

I nod, grateful for Charlie's unwavering support. "You're right. So, what's next on that list of yours?"

We spend the next hour going over Charlie's extremely detailed plans. By the time we leave the diner, my head is spinning with to-do lists and timelines. But there's also a spark of excitement building in my chest. Maybe this viewing party won't be so bad after all.

That afternoon, I find myself at the local hardware store, picking up supplies for some minor repairs around the house. As I'm examining different types of wood filler for that creaky floorboard, I hear a familiar voice behind me.

"Well, if it isn't Lena Larson, beautiful hostess extraordinaire."

I turn to see Sheriff Mark with a friendly smile on his face. He looks as handsome as ever in his uniform, in spite of the early hour.

"Hi, Mark," I greet him, returning his smile. "News travels fast, huh?"

He chuckles. "Small town, remember? I hear you're opening up your home for Marianne Olsen's big Hollywood shindig."

"Viewing party," I correct him. "It's just a small gathering to watch her new movie. Nothing too fancy."

Mark raises an eyebrow. "A Hollywood star coming back to her hometown for a premiere? Sounds pretty fancy to me. You need any help with security or anything?"

I'm about to decline when a thought strikes me. "Actually, there is something you might be able to help with. Do you remember James Peterson?"

Mark's expression turns serious. "Herald Peterson's son? Yeah, I remember him. Why do you ask?"

I hesitate, unsure how to explain the uneasy feeling I got from my encounter with James. "I ran into him at the grocery store yesterday. He said some... strange things. About secrets coming to light. I don't know, it just felt... off."

Mark frowns. "James has been through a lot since his father's death. He's never caused any trouble, but I'll keep an eye on him. Thanks for the heads up."

As we chat a bit more about the upcoming event, I can't help but feel a sense of relief. Having the sheriff on alert eases some of my worries about James. But there's still a nagging feeling in the pit of my stomach, a sense that there's more going on than meets the eye.

Back at home, I'm in the middle of touching up some paint in the living room when the temperature suddenly drops. I don't need to turn around to know that Granny's ghost has materialized.

"Lena, dear," her spectral voice calls out. "We need to talk about this viewing party of yours."

I sigh, putting down my paintbrush. "Granny, we've been over this. It's just a small gathering. Nothing to worry about."

But as I turn to face her, the grave expression on her translucent face makes me pause. Granny's ghost is floating near the fireplace, her form shimmering slightly in the afternoon light.

"It's not the party itself I'm worried about," she says, her voice taking on that eerie echo it gets when she's particularly concerned. "It's what it might bring to light. There are things about this town, about your family, that have been buried for a long time. Marianne's return could stir up more than just old high school rivalries."

I feel a chill that has nothing to do with Granny's ghostly presence. "What do you mean? What things?"

Granny's form flickers, a sign of her agitation. "I can't say more. The veil between worlds... it obscures some things. But be careful, Lena. Keep your eyes open. And whatever you do, don't trust everything you see."

Before I can ask any more questions, Granny's ghost fades away, leaving me alone in the suddenly too-quiet house. I sink onto the couch, my mind reeling. Between James's cryptic comments and now Granny's warning, what should have been a simple viewing party is starting to feel like the beginning of something much bigger.

The next few days pass in a whirlwind of activity. Charlie and I throw ourselves into preparations for the viewing party, cleaning every nook and cranny of my house, rearranging furniture, and debating endlessly about the perfect snacks to serve.

"Do you think we need caviar?" Charlie asks one afternoon, flipping through a gourmet food magazine. "That seems like something a Hollywood star would expect, right?"

I laugh, shaking my head. "Charlie, this is New Oslo, not Beverly Hills. I think we can stick to good old-fashioned popcorn and maybe some of Betty's famous mini quiches."

As the day of the viewing party draws nearer, the excitement in town reaches a fever pitch. It seems like everywhere I go, people are talking about Marianne Olsen and her triumphant return.

The morning of the viewing party dawns bright and clear. I'm up with the sun, too nervous to sleep any longer. As I'm making a final sweep through the house, making sure everything is perfect, I hear a knock at the door.

I suck in a sharp breath. It's too early for Charlie or any of the other guests. Could it be...?

I open the door to find Marianne Olsen standing on my porch, looking every inch the Hollywood star. Her blonde hair is perfectly styled, her makeup flawless, and she's wearing an outfit that probably costs more than my entire wardrobe.

"Lena," she says, her voice cool and composed. "It's been a long time."

As I stand there, frozen in surprise, I can't help but think: the viewing party hasn't even started yet, and already, things are not going according to plan. With Marianne's early arrival, I have a feeling this day is going to be full of unexpected twists and turns. And as I invite her in, I can almost hear Granny's ghostly voice whispering a warning in my ear.

Chapter 3

Marianne's early arrival throws me off balance, but I don't have time to dwell on it. Within minutes of ushering her into the house, my doorbell starts ringing nonstop. The guests have begun to arrive, and I find myself swept up in a whirlwind of greetings and introductions.

Mayor Robert Swenson is one of the first to arrive, his wife Margaret in tow. They're dressed to the nines, clearly viewing this as New Oslo's social event of the year. The mayor's eyes gleam with poorly concealed excitement as he shakes Marianne's hand, no doubt already planning how to use this brush with celebrity to his political advantage.

"Marianne, darling!" a voice booms from the doorway. A man in an impeccably tailored suit strides in, sunglasses perched on his head despite the fact that the sun set an hour ago. "Traffic was a nightmare. I told you we should have gotten a helicopter!"

Marianne rolls her eyes, but there's a fond smile on her face. "Everyone," she says, addressing the room at large, "this is my agent, Samuel Goodson."

Samuel surveys the room with a critical eye, his gaze lingering on the snack table Charlie and I painstakingly arranged. I can almost see him mentally replacing our carefully curated selection of local delicacies with caviar and champagne.

More guests filter in: the high school principal, the owner of the local paper, and several of Marianne's old classmates, all trying a bit too hard to appear nonchalant about rubbing elbows with a celebrity.

Just as I'm beginning to feel overwhelmed by the crush of people, the doorbell rings once more. I open it to find a young man with movie-star good looks and a dazzling smile.

"Hi, I'm Jake," he says, extending his hand. "Marianne's boyfriend. Sorry I'm late—had to make sure her surprise was perfect."

Before I can ask what surprise he's referring to, Marianne appears at my side, throwing her arms around Jake. "You made it!" she exclaims, planting a kiss on his cheek.

As I watch them together, a pang of something—nostalgia? envy?—hits me. They look like the perfect Hollywood couple, all gleaming smiles and easy affection. It's a stark reminder of how different Marianne's life is now from the rest of us in New Oslo.

With all the guests arrived, there's a palpable buzz of excitement in the air. My living room, usually so spacious, feels cramped with bodies. The hum of conversation is punctuated by the occasional flash of a camera or the ring of laughter.

Suddenly, Samuel the agent claps his hands, calling for attention. "Ladies and gentlemen," he announces, "the woman of the hour would like to say a few words before we start the movie."

The room falls silent as Marianne takes center stage, positioning herself in front of the large screen we've set up for the viewing. In the soft lamplight, she looks almost ethereal, her blonde hair glowing like a halo around her face.

"First of all," she begins, her voice clear and confident, "I want to thank everyone for coming tonight. And a special thank you to Lena for opening her beautiful home to us." She flashes me a smile that seems genuine, and for a moment, I see a flicker of the girl I once knew.

"You know," Marianne continues, her tone becoming more reflective, "when I left New Oslo all those years ago, I had big dreams and even bigger insecurities. I was just a small-town girl with stars in her eyes, determined to make it in Hollywood."

She pauses, her gaze sweeping across the room. "The journey wasn't easy. There were plenty of times I thought about giving up, about coming back home with my tail between my legs. But every time I felt like quitting, I remembered something my drama teacher, Mrs. Samson, used to say: 'In every small town, there's a story waiting to be told.'"

I see Mrs. Samson in the corner, dabbing at her eyes with a tissue. Marianne's words seem to have struck a chord with many in the room. Even Charlie, standing beside me, looks moved.

"That's what kept me going," Marianne says, her voice thick with emotion. "The desire to tell stories—not just my own, but the stories of places like New Oslo. Of people like all of you. All of us. And that's what this movie is about. Some people say it might be just another horror flick, but I like to think of it as a love letter to small towns everywhere, to the dreams they inspire and the secrets they keep."

She takes a deep breath, and I can see tears glistening in her eyes. "I know I wasn't always the easiest person to get along with in high school," she admits, and I feel my eyebrows raise in surprise at this unexpected candor. "I was scared and insecure, and I didn't always handle those feelings well. But being away... it's given me perspective. It's made me appreciate where I came from, and the people who shaped me, for better or worse."

Marianne's gaze finds mine, and I'm startled by the sincerity I see there. "I hope this movie makes you all proud. I know I can say without a doubt that I'm proud of the work I did in it."

As Marianne concludes her speech, the room erupts in applause. I find myself clapping along, moved despite my lingering reservations. Maybe Charlie was right. Maybe people really can change.

With the speech over, everyone settles in for the main event. The lights dim, and a hush falls over the room as the opening credits roll. I curl up in my favorite armchair, a bowl of popcorn balanced on my lap, and prepare to watch Marianne's big Hollywood debut.

The movie, it turns out, is a suspenseful horror film set in a small town not unlike New Oslo. As the plot unfolds, I find myself drawn in despite my usual aversion to scary movies. The story follows a young woman who returns to her hometown after years away, only to uncover a web of dark secrets and hidden dangers.

I can't help but draw parallels between the protagonist and Marianne. Is this how she sees New Oslo? As a place full of sinister undercurrents and buried truths? The thought makes me shiver, and I pull my cardigan tighter around me.

The tension in the room builds as the movie progresses. I can hear gasps and nervous laughter from the other guests as the scares mount. Even Charlie, usually unflappable, jumps at a particularly shocking moment, nearly spilling her drink.

As we near what is clearly the climax of the film, I find myself on the edge of my seat. The fictional, on-screen version of Marianne is creeping through a dark house, searching for the truth that will unravel the town's mysteries. The music swells, building to a crescendo. On screen, a shadowy figure appears behind our unsuspecting leading lady, raising a knife...

And suddenly, we're plunged into darkness.

The power cuts out with a decisive snap, leaving us in total darkness. For a moment, there's silence, as if everyone is holding their breath, waiting for the lights to flicker back on. But they don't.

My nose starts to twitch, a sure sign that something bad is about to happen.

Then, a blood-curdling scream pierces the air.

Chaos erupts. I can hear people stumbling around in the dark, voices raised in panic and confusion. Someone knocks over a lamp, the crash of breaking glass adding to the cacophony.

"Everyone, please stay calm!" I hear Mayor Swenson shout, but his voice is drowned out by the rising tide of panic.

I fumble in my pocket for my phone, hoping to use it as a flashlight. My hands are shaking so badly I nearly drop it. As I finally manage to turn on the light, a ghostly chill sweeps through the room. For a moment, I think I see Granny's spectral form flickering in the corner, her face a mask of concern.

But before I can process this, the emergency generator kicks in. Battery-powered lights flicker to life, casting an eerie glow over the scene.

And that's when I see her.

Marianne is sprawled on the floor in front of the screen, her blonde hair fanned out around her like a broken halo. Her eyes are wide open, staring sightlessly at the ceiling. And protruding from her chest, gleaming wickedly in the dim light, is a butcher knife.

The scream that rips from my own throat is primal, born of shock and horror. Around me, I can hear similar cries of dismay as others take in the gruesome scene.

Samuel, Marianne's agent, pushes through the crowd, falling to his knees beside her. "Marianne! Oh God, Marianne!" he wails, reaching out as if to touch her, then pulling back at the last moment.

Jake, Marianne's boyfriend, stands frozen a few feet away, his face a mask of disbelief. "This... this can't be happening," he mutters, over and over again.

I feel Charlie's hand on my arm, gripping tightly. "Lena," she whispers, her voice shaking, "what do we do?"

But I can't answer. I can't move. I can't think. All I can do is stare at the body of Marianne Olsen, the small-town girl turned Hollywood star, whose homecoming has turned into a nightmare.

As the reality of the situation sinks in, one thought cuts through the fog of shock and horror in my mind: This isn't just a tragedy. It's a crime. And it happened in my house, under my watch.

The viewing party has become a crime scene. And every person in this room, myself included, is now a potential suspect.

Chapter 4

The shock of discovering Marianne's body threatens to overwhelm me, but a sudden squeeze of my arm jolts me back to reality. It's Charlie, her face pale but determined.

"Lena," she whispers urgently, "we need to do something. Now."

She's right, of course. I take a deep breath, forcing myself to think clearly. The room is still in chaos, people milling about in confusion and horror. If we don't act quickly, any evidence could be destroyed.

"Okay," I say, my voice sounding strangely calm to my own ears. "You take the left side of the room, I'll take the right. We need to get everyone away from... from Marianne."

Charlie nods, immediately moving to herd a group of shell-shocked guests toward the dining room. I turn to the rest of the crowd, raising my voice to be heard over the commotion.

"Everyone, please!" I call out. "I know this is shocking, but we need to clear the area. Please move to the dining room or the front porch. Don't leave the property and don't touch anything!"

To my surprise, people begin to listen. Maybe it's the authoritative tone in my voice, or maybe they're just relieved to have someone telling them what to do. Slowly but surely, the living room begins to empty.

I spot Jake, Marianne's boyfriend, still standing frozen near her body. Gently, I approach him. "Jake," I say softly, "I'm so sorry, but we need to secure the area. Can you wait in the dining room? I promise we'll get to the bottom of this."

He looks at me with vacant eyes, nodding mechanically before allowing me to guide him out of the room. As I turn back, I see Samuel, the agent, kneeling beside Marianne, sobbing uncontrollably.

"Samuel," I say, trying to keep my voice steady, "I know this is hard, but we can't disturb anything. The police will be here soon. Please, let's step away."

For a moment, I think he's going to refuse. But then he nods, stumbling to his feet and allowing Charlie to lead him away.

Finally, the room is clear except for Charlie and me. We exchange a grim look. "I've called Sheriff Mark," Charlie says. "He's on his way."

I nod, grateful for her quick thinking. "Now we wait," I say, trying to ignore the lifeless form on my living room floor. "And we make sure no one comes back in here."

The wait for Sheriff Mark feels interminable, though in reality it's probably only about ten minutes. When I hear the wail of sirens approaching, relief washes over me. Help is here. Professionals who will know what to do, who will make sense of this senseless act.

The front door bursts open, and Sheriff Mark strides in, flanked by two deputies. His eyes widen as he takes in the scene, but his voice is calm and authoritative when he speaks.

"Lena, Charlie," he nods to us. "You did the right thing clearing the room. Now, I need you to tell me exactly what happened."

As Charlie and I take turns explaining the events of the evening, the deputies begin to cordon off the area with yellow crime scene tape. It's surreal, watching my living room transform into a crime scene for the third time in the past year. Why does this sort of thing keep happening to me? And why here, of all places?

"Alright," Sheriff Mark says when we finish our account. "We'll need to question everyone who was here. Can you help my deputies get everyone organized? We'll use the dining room as a temporary interview area."

I nod, grateful for something concrete to do. As Charlie and I begin to herd the guests back inside for questioning, I can't help but scan the room, looking for... what? Clues? Evidence? I'm not sure, but something compels me to take in every detail.

That's when I start to notice things. Small things, details that might mean nothing, but which stand out in the unnaturally still room. There's a vase on the side table that's been knocked over, water seeping into the antique wood. I don't remember bumping into it, and I'm usually so careful with my grandmother's heirlooms.

My eyes travel to the wall near where Marianne fell. There's a smudge there, just at shoulder height. It could be nothing—guests had been mingling all evening, after all. But something about it catches my attention. It's not just a casual brush against the wall. It looks more like someone braced themselves against it forcefully.

And then there's Marianne herself. I force myself to look at her, really look at her, pushing past the horror of the knife in her chest. She's wearing the same outfit she arrived in, a stylish dress that probably cost more than my entire wardrobe. But something's missing. I remember she was wearing a necklace earlier in the evening—a delicate gold chain with a small pendant. Now, her neck is bare.

I'm about to mention these observations to Sheriff Mark when a familiar chill sweeps through the room. I turn, knowing what I'll see before I see it. Granny's ghost has materialized in the corner, her spectral form flickering in agitation.

"Lena," she says, her voice echoing slightly in that way it does when she's particularly upset. "This is worse than I feared."

I glance around, making sure no one is paying attention to me before I whisper, "Granny, what are you doing here?"

"Helping," she says firmly. "Or at least, I'm going to try. I may not be able to touch things in your world, but I can keep my eyes and ears open. No one will suspect a ghost of spying."

I feel a rush of gratitude. Having Granny on my side, even if she is incorporeal, is comforting. "Thank you," I murmur. "Just... be careful, okay?"

Granny's form shimmers, which I've come to recognize as her version of a nod. "You be careful too, dear. Remember, not everything is as it seems."

Before I can ask what she means by that cryptic statement, a commotion from the dining room draws my attention. I hurry toward the noise, Granny's ghost fading from view behind me.

The scene that greets me in the dining room is one of barely contained chaos. Samuel is on his feet, his face red with anger and grief. He's pointing accusingly at various guests, his voice rising to a shout.

"It was one of you!" he yells. "You were all jealous of her! She made it out of this backwater town, she became a star, and you couldn't stand it!"

Sheriff Mark tries to calm him down, but Samuel is beyond reason. "Was it you?" he demands, rounding on Mayor Swenson. "Worried she'd spill some dirty secrets about your precious town? Or you?" He turns to Jake. "Afraid she was going to leave you behind when she hit the big time?"

Jake stands up, his face twisted with grief and anger. "How dare you!" he shouts. "I loved Marianne! I would never—"

"Enough!" Sheriff Mark's voice cuts through the argument. "Mr. Goodson, I understand you're upset, but throwing accusations around isn't helping anyone. We will get to the bottom of this, but I need everyone to remain calm and cooperative."

Samuel slumps back into his chair, burying his face in his hands. The room falls into an uneasy silence, but I can feel the tension crackling in the air like electricity before a storm.

As the night wears on and the questioning continues, that tension only grows. Old resentments and rivalries that I thought had been long buried begin to surface. I overhear snippets of conversations that make my stomach churn.

"Well, she always did think she was better than the rest of us," I hear someone mutter. "Guess Hollywood didn't change that."

In another corner, I see Tyler Hanson, Marianne's ex-boyfriend from high school, engaged in a heated whispered argument with his wife. "I told you nothing happened!" he hisses. "It was just a few emails, that's all!"

Even Mayor Swenson seems on edge, his usual political smoothness cracking under the strain. When one of the deputies asks him about his whereabouts during the blackout, he stumbles over his words, something I've never seen him do before.

As I watch all this unfold, a sick feeling grows in the pit of my stomach. These are people I've known my whole life. Neighbors, friends, pillars of the community. And yet, looking at them now, I realize I don't really know them at all. Any one of them could be a killer.

Chapter 5

Once he seems certain the crime scene is secure, Sheriff Mark sets up a makeshift interview area in my study. The room, usually a haven of peace and quiet, now feels charged with tension. I watch as he settles into my grandfather's old leather chair, a notepad in hand and a grim expression on his face.

"Okay, Lena," he says, catching my eye. "I'm going to start interviewing everyone. I know you and Charlie want to help, but I need you to stay out of the way. Let me handle this."

I nod, trying to look compliant, but inside my mind is racing. There's no way I'm going to sit idly by while a killer roams free in my home. I catch Charlie's eye and give her a subtle nod. She returns it, understanding passing between us without a word. We might not be able to conduct interviews ourselves, but that doesn't mean we can't listen.

As Sheriff Mark calls in the first guest, Charlie and I position ourselves in the hallway, just out of sight but within earshot. It's not the most comfortable spot, crouched behind a large potted fern, but it gives us a perfect vantage point to eavesdrop on the interviews.

The first few interviews yield little of interest. Mrs. Johnson swears she was in the bathroom when the lights went out. Mr. Looper claims he was refilling his drink in the kitchen. Plausible alibis, but impossible to verify in the chaos that followed the blackout.

It's when James Peterson takes the seat across from Sheriff Mark that things start to get interesting. From my hiding spot, I can see James fidgeting, his usual cool demeanor cracking under the sheriff's steady gaze.

"Mr. Peterson," Sheriff Mark begins, "can you tell me where you were when the power went out?"

James clears his throat. "I was, uh, by the snack table. Getting some of those little quiches."

"And did you see or hear anything unusual before the lights went out?" Sheriff Mark presses.

James hesitates, just a fraction too long. "No, nothing. It all happened so fast, you know?"

But there's something in his voice, a hint of uncertainty that makes me wonder. I remember our encounter at the grocery store, his cryptic words about secrets coming to light. Could James be involved in this somehow?

As James leaves the study, looking relieved to be done with questioning, I can't shake the feeling that he's hiding something. But before I can dwell on it, the next interview captures my attention.

Mayor Swenson enters the study, his usual confident stride replaced by a nervous shuffle. As Sheriff Mark begins his questioning, the mayor's political smooth talk seems to desert him.

"Mayor Swenson," Sheriff Mark says, his tone deceptively casual, "I understand you and Ms. Olsen had some business dealings recently?"

The mayor's face pales visibly. "I... well, yes. But it was nothing, really. Just a small investment opportunity she approached me about."

"An investment opportunity?" Sheriff Mark raises an eyebrow. "Can you elaborate?"

The mayor shifts uncomfortably in his seat. "Marianne had this idea for a reality TV show. 'Small Town Secrets' or something like that. She wanted to film it here in New Oslo. Said it would put us on the map, bring in tourism."

I feel my eyes widen in surprise. A reality show set in New Oslo? The idea seems absurd.

"And what happened with this show idea?" Sheriff Mark prompts.

The mayor's discomfort is palpable now. "It... well, it fell through. The network wasn't interested. But Marianne had already used some of the investment money for development. She said she'd pay it back, but..."

He trails off, but the implication is clear. Marianne owed the mayor money, money that he might never see again now that she's dead. It's not a motive for murder, exactly, but it's certainly something the mayor had reason to be angry about.

As the mayor leaves, looking shaken, Charlie and I exchange meaningful glances. The plot, as they say, thickens.

The next interview proves even more revealing. Tyler Hanson, Marianne's high school ex-boyfriend and now a teacher at New Oslo High, takes the hot seat. I remember overhearing his argument with his wife earlier, about emails exchanged with Marianne.

Sheriff Mark doesn't beat around the bush. "Mr. Hanson, we've been informed that you've been in recent contact with Ms. Olsen. Can you tell me about that?"

Tyler's face flushes red. "It was nothing, really. Just... catching up."

"Catching up?" Sheriff Mark's tone is skeptical. "We have reason to believe the emails were somewhat less than friendly. Care to explain?"

Tyler slumps in his chair, the fight going out of him. "Okay, look. When Marianne got in touch about coming back to New Oslo, she... she suggested we might pick up where we left off in high school. I told her I was married now, happily married. She didn't take it well."

I feel a rush of sympathy for Tyler's wife, followed quickly by a surge of anger at Marianne. It seems her return to New Oslo was stirring up more trouble than anyone realized.

"Did you send her any angry emails in response?" Sheriff Mark asks.

Tyler nods miserably. "I told her to leave me alone, to stop trying to mess up my life. I was pretty harsh, I guess. But I swear, I'd never hurt her. Not physically, anyway."

As Tyler leaves, I can't help but wonder how many other lives Marianne had tried to disrupt with her return. How many other potential enemies had she made?

The interviews continue, each one revealing new layers of complexity to the case. But it's when Samuel Goodson, Marianne's agent, takes his turn that things really get interesting.

I listen intently as Sheriff Mark questions him about his movements at the time of the murder. But something strange happens. With each retelling, Samuel's story seems to change slightly. First, he says he was by the fireplace when the lights went out. Then, he mentions being near the kitchen. Later still, he claims he was right next to Marianne.

Charlie nudges me, whispering, "Is it just me, or is his story getting more inconsistent with each telling?"

I nod, a knot forming in my stomach. Why would Samuel be lying? What does he have to hide?

As the night wears on, my head spins with all the new information. It seems like everyone had some sort of connection to Marianne, some reason to potentially want her out of the picture. But who actually did it? Who hated her enough to plunge a knife into her chest?

It's late when I finally get a moment alone. The police have finished their initial sweep of the house, and most of the guests have been allowed to leave, though they've been warned not to leave town. I find myself drawn back to the living room, the scene of the crime.

Yellow police tape crisscrosses the room, turning my cozy home into something out of a TV crime drama. Marianne's body has been taken away, but I can still see the outline where she fell, marked in chalk on my hardwood floor.

My eyes fall on Marianne's purse, still sitting on the side table where she left it. The police have already gone through it, of course, but something compels me to take a closer look. Maybe it's Granny's influence, her ghostly voice in my head urging me to leave no stone unturned.

Glancing around to make sure I'm alone, I gingerly open the purse. Most of its contents are unremarkable—makeup, a wallet, a phone with a cracked screen. But as I'm about to give up, my fingers brush against something crumpled at the bottom of the bag.

I pull it out carefully. It's a note, written on expensive-looking stationery and crushed into a ball as if in anger. With trembling hands, I smooth it out, my eyes widening as I read the words scrawled across the page:

"I know what you did. If you don't want everyone else to know too, meet me at midnight. Come alone, or everything gets exposed."

The note isn't signed, but its implications are clear. Someone was blackmailing Marianne. But who? And what secret were they holding over her head?

As I stare at the note, my mind reeling, I hear footsteps approaching. Quickly, I shove the paper into my pocket, just as Mark appears in the doorway.

"Lena? You okay?" he asks, concern etched on his face.

I force a smile, trying to look casual. "Yeah, just... taking it all in, I guess."

But inside, my thoughts are racing. This note changes everything. It's not just about old grudges or soured business deals anymore. There's a deeper, darker secret at play here. And finding out what it is might be the key to solving Marianne's murder.

Chapter 6

It's early in the morning, but I've been awake for hours. I can't stop tossing and turning, my mind a whirlwind of fragmented memories from last night. Marianne's lifeless eyes, the chaos that erupted when the lights came back on, the shrill sound of Samuel Goodson's accusations—it all blends into a nightmarish kaleidoscope that refuses to settle.

With a sigh, I push myself out of bed, knowing sleep won't come again. I pad downstairs, my bare feet silent on the cool wooden floors, and head straight for the kitchen. The familiar ritual of brewing coffee provides a small sense of normalcy, something to anchor me in this sea of uncertainty.

As the rich aroma of coffee fills the air, I reach for my phone and dial Charlie's number. It rings twice before her sleep-roughened voice answers.

"Lena? Everything okay?"

"As okay as it can be, given the circumstances," I reply, pouring myself a steaming cup. "Listen, can you come over for breakfast? I think we need to talk through everything that happened last night."

There's a rustling sound on the other end, and I can picture Charlie sitting up in bed, running a hand through her short, perpetually messy hair. "Yeah, of course. Give me twenty minutes?"

"Perfect. I'll whip up some pancakes."

By the time Charlie arrives, looking rumpled but alert, I've managed to create a spread of blueberry pancakes, crispy bacon, and fresh fruit. It's probably more food than either of us will be able to eat, but the act of cooking has helped calm my nerves.

"Wow, you've been busy," Charlie says, eyeing the feast as she hangs her jacket on the back of a kitchen chair.

I shrug, sliding a plate toward her. "Couldn't sleep. Figured I might as well do something productive."

We settle into a comfortable silence as we begin to eat, the weight of last night's events hanging heavy in the air between us. I'm about halfway through my second pancake when a familiar chill runs down my spine. I look up to see Granny Ingrid's translucent form materializing near the kitchen counter.

"Oh," I say, setting down my fork. "Granny's here."

Charlie glances up from her plate, her eyes scanning the empty space where I'm looking. She can't see Granny, but she's known about my spectral visitor long enough to take it in stride. "Morning, Granny," she says casually, speaking to the air. "What's she saying, Lena?"

"Good morning, dears," Granny says, her voice carrying that slight echo that I've come to associate with her ghostly presence. "I hope you don't mind me joining your little breakfast meeting."

I relay Granny's greeting to Charlie, who nods, unsurprised. Despite the unconventional nature of our three-way conversations, Charlie's acceptance of my unusual ability has always been a source of comfort.

"Not at all, Granny," I say, gesturing to an empty chair. "We could use your insight." I turn to Charlie. "Granny's going to sit with us."

As Granny settles into her seat, I push my plate aside and lean forward, my elbows on the table. "Okay, let's review what we know so far. Charlie, what stood out to you from our little eavesdropping session last night?"

Charlie swallows her mouthful of food and nods, her expression turning serious. "Well, there were quite a few inconsistencies in people's stories. James Peterson, for one. He claimed he was in several different spots at once when the lights went out."

I nod, recalling my own observations. "And let's not forget Mayor Swenson. He was awfully quick to point fingers at others, wasn't he? Almost like he was trying to deflect attention from himself."

"Oh, that Mayor Swenson," Granny Ingrid chimes in, her ghostly eyes narrowing. "He's always been a slippery one, even back in my day. Wouldn't surprise me if he had something to hide."

I relay Granny's comments to Charlie, who raises an eyebrow. "Granny's got a point. The mayor did seem particularly nervous."

Charlie leans back in her chair, a thoughtful look on her face. "Then there's Tyler Hanson. Marianne's high school sweetheart turned local teacher. He seemed genuinely shocked by her death, but those angry emails he sent her recently... that's not nothing."

I bite my lip, remembering the crumpled note I found in Marianne's purse. "Speaking of communications," I say slowly, reaching into my pocket and pulling out the carefully smoothed piece of paper. "I found this in Marianne's purse last night. I think... I think she was being blackmailed."

Charlie's eyes widen as I place the note on the table. Granny leans in, her spectral form shimmering slightly as she focuses on the words.

Charlie reads the note aloud, keeping her voice low. "Well, that's certainly ominous. Any idea who might have sent it?"

I shake my head, frustration bubbling up inside me. "No clue. Marianne always seemed to have it all together, at least on the surface. But clearly, there was more going on beneath that perfect facade."

Granny Ingrid makes a soft humming sound, a habit she's retained even in her ghostly state. "Keep in mind, dears, Marianne wasn't always the polished starlet we all saw last night. I remember her as a young girl, always getting into scrapes and causing mischief. Then of course you both remember how she was in high school."

I lean forward, intrigued, and quickly relay Granny's words to Charlie. "Really, Granny? What kind of mischief?"

As Granny begins to speak, I translate for Charlie, our eyes meeting in shared curiosity. Granny's eyes take on a faraway look, as if she's peering into the past. "Oh, nothing too serious at first. Sneaking out after curfew, pulling pranks on her classmates. But as she got older, the stakes seemed to get higher. Remember that incident during your senior year of high school? Something about a fire at the old boathouse by the lake? Nothing was ever proven, of course, but I can remember rumors flying for months."

Charlie and I exchange glances, our minds racing with the implications. I vaguely remember the incident Granny mentioned, but we were kids back then. We didn't really pay much attention to the news.

"And her relationships," Granny continues, her voice taking on a gossipy tone that makes me smile despite the gravity of the situation. I quickly summarize for Charlie as Granny speaks. "That girl left a trail of broken hearts wherever she went. Not just

Tyler Hanson, mind you. There were others, some of them... well, let's just say they weren't exactly single at the time."

The pieces are starting to come together in my mind, forming a picture of Marianne that's far more complex than I'd initially thought. I'm about to ask Granny for more details when the sound of a car pulling up outside catches my attention.

Charlie is on her feet in an instant, peering out the kitchen window. "It's Sheriff Mark," she says, turning back to me with a puzzled expression. "What's he doing here so early?"

Before I can respond, there's a sharp knock at the front door. I hurry to answer it, my heart pounding with a mixture of anticipation and dread. Sheriff Mark stands on my porch, his handsome face creased with worry.

"Morning, Lena," he says, tipping his hat. "Sorry to bother you so early, but we've got some new information I thought you might be interested in hearing."

I almost smile. There was a time not too long ago when the sheriff would've insisted I stay out of his investigations. Now he's making a special trip over here to share evidence. Things have certainly changed in the few months we've been dating off and on.

I step back, gesturing for him to come in. "Of course, Mark. What is it?"

He follows me into the kitchen, nodding a greeting to Charlie. If he notices me glancing at the empty chair where Granny's invisible form sits, he doesn't mention it.

"The forensics team finished their preliminary examination of the murder weapon," He says, his voice grave. "They found fingerprints on the handle of the knife."

For a moment, hope surges through me. Could it be that simple? But then I see the troubled look in Mark's eyes, and I know there's more to it.

"The thing is," he continues, "those prints don't match anyone who was at the party last night. Not a single guest, not the catering staff, not even you or Charlie."

The implications of this new information hit me like a physical blow. An unknown person, someone who wasn't on any guest list or staff roster, had been in my house last night. Had been there when Marianne was killed.

As I sink into a chair, my mind reeling, I catch a glimpse of Granny Ingrid's face. Her spectral features are set in a grim expression that sends a chill down my spine. I look at Charlie, seeing my own shock and confusion mirrored in her eyes. Whatever is going on here, I have a feeling it's far more complicated—and dangerous—than any of us initially thought.

Chapter 7

We've been poring over witness statements for what feels like forever, and our coffee has long since gone cold. My eyes ache from the strain of reading cramped handwriting and official police forms, but I force myself to focus. Somewhere in this mess of paper is the key to understanding what happened to Marianne.

"Lena, look at this," Charlie says, sliding a statement across the table to me. Her finger points to a name that makes my stomach clench: James Peterson.

"We should talk to him," I say, standing up so abruptly that my chair scrapes loudly against the floor. "His mom, too. He was at the premiere with us, but she would've been right next door the whole time. If anyone saw or heard anything suspicious that night, it would be Mrs. Peterson."

Charlie looks uncertain. "Are you sure that's a good idea? I mean, given the history..."

I know we're both thinking the same thing. James has held a grudge against me and my family ever since his dad was killed in connection with my Granny Ingrid's murder.

I shake my head, cutting her off. "We have to. This isn't about old grudges or family history. This is about finding out what happened to Marianne."

As we walk the short distance to the Peterson house, I can't help but feel a sense of unease. The last time I spoke to James was at his father's funeral, and that was a scene I'd rather forget.

We're halfway up the front walk when we hear raised voices coming from inside the house. Charlie and I exchange a glance, slowing our pace. As we get closer, the words become clearer.

"...can't keep doing this, James!" It's a woman's voice, tense and worried. James's mother, I realize with a start.

"I don't have a choice!" James's voice, angry and defensive. "Do you think I wanted any of this?"

"But what if someone finds out? What if-"

"No one's going to find out," James cuts her off. "I'll make sure of it."

There's a moment of tense silence, and then his mother's voice again, softer this time. "Fine. I'll... I'll take care of any loose ends. But James, promise me this is the end of it."

My heart is pounding so hard I'm sure Charlie must be able to hear it. I look at her, seeing my own shock and confusion mirrored in her eyes. Before we can decide what to do, the decision is made for us. The front door swings open, revealing James's mother.

She looks startled to see us standing there, her eyes wide and nervous. She's wearing a light sweater despite the warm weather, and I notice her hands are shaking slightly as she grips the door frame.

"Lena? Charlie?" she says, her voice pitched higher than normal. "What are you doing here?"

I clear my throat, trying to find my voice. "Mrs. Peterson, we're sorry to bother you. We were hoping we could ask you a few questions about the night of the party at my house."

She glances over her shoulder, then back at us, her expression growing more anxious by the second. "I... I'm not sure this is a good time. Perhaps you could come back later?"

Before I can respond, I hear James's voice from inside the house. "Who is it, Mom?"

Mrs. Peterson hesitates, but James doesn't wait for an answer. I hear his footsteps approaching, and then he's there, looming behind his mother in the doorway. His eyes narrow when he sees me.

"What are you doing here, Lena?" he asks, his voice cold. "You need to leave. Now."

The hostility in his voice takes me aback, even though I should have expected it. In that moment, I'm transported back to last year, standing in the cemetery as they lowered Harold's casket into the ground. I remember approaching James afterward, my throat tight with grief and guilt.

"James, I'm so sorry," I had said, reaching out to touch his arm. He had jerked away as if my touch burned him, his eyes blazing with a fury that made me take a step back.

"Sorry?" he had spat. "Your family is the reason my dad is dead. Don't you dare say you're sorry."

Now, standing on his front porch, I see that same anger in his eyes. It hasn't diminished in the slightest over the past year. If anything, it seems to have grown, festering like an open wound.

I swallow hard, forcing myself to meet his gaze. "James, we're just trying to understand what happened to Marianne. If anyone saw or heard anything that night, or—"

"My mom didn't see anything," he cuts me off. "And even if she had, why would we tell you? You're not the police, Lena. You're just a nosy neighbor who can't mind her own business."

His words sting, but I try not to let it show. "James, please. Marianne was murdered. Don't you want to know what happened?"

For a moment, something flickers in James's eyes, but it's gone so quickly I can't be sure I saw it at all. "What I want," he says slowly, "is for you to leave me and my mother alone. We've got nothing to say to you."

I open my mouth to argue, but Charlie puts a hand on my arm, shaking her head slightly. I sigh, knowing she's right. Pushing further now will only make things worse.

"We understand," Charlie says, keeping her voice calm and professional. "Thank you for your time, Mrs. Peterson, James. If you think of anything that might be helpful, please don't hesitate to contact us or the sheriff's office."

Mrs. Peterson nods, relief evident on her face. "Of course. Good day, girls."

The door closes firmly, leaving Charlie and me standing on the porch, staring at each other in stunned silence. Slowly, we make our way back to my house, neither of us speaking until we're safely inside with the door closed behind us.

"Well," Charlie says finally, "that was..."

"Weird?" I supply. "Suspicious? Completely unhelpful?"

"All of the above," Charlie agrees. She runs a hand through her hair, a habit she's had since we were kids. "What do you think they were arguing about when we walked up? Those 'loose ends' his mother mentioned?"

I shake my head, frustration building inside me. "I don't know, but it's a heck of a coincidence, isn't it? The murder happens right next door, and suddenly James and his mom are having heated arguments about secrets and loose ends?"

Charlie nods slowly. "It definitely raises some red flags. But Lena," she hesitates, giving me a concerned look, "you know we have to consider the possibility that this isn't related to Marianne at all. It could be about... well, about what happened last year."

I sink into a chair, suddenly feeling exhausted. Charlie's right, of course. The timing of Marianne's murder and this suspicious behavior from the Petersons could be nothing more than an unfortunate coincidence.

"You're right," I admit. "We can't jump to conclusions. But Charlie, I can't ignore this either. There's something going on with the Petersons, and I intend to find out what it is."

Charlie sits down across from me, her expression serious. "I'm with you, Lena. Whatever's going on, we'll figure it out together. But we need to be careful. If James is involved in something dangerous..."

She doesn't finish the thought, but she doesn't need to. I know the risks we're taking by investigating this on our own. But as I think about Marianne, about my grandmother, about Harold Peterson, I know I don't have a choice. Too many lives have been destroyed already.

"We'll be careful," I promise Charlie. "But we're not giving up. Marianne deserves justice, and if the Petersons know something that can help us find her killer, we're going to find out what it is."

As I say the words, I feel a familiar chill run down my spine. I look up, half-expecting to see Granny Ingrid's ghost materializing in the kitchen. But the room remains empty, save for Charlie and me. Still, I can't shake the feeling that my grandmother is with us somehow, urging us forward in our investigation.

With renewed determination, Charlie and I turn back to our pile of witness statements.

Chapter 8

The streets of New Oslo are quieter than usual as Charlie and I make our way downtown. It's like there's an undercurrent of tension running through the town in the wake of Marianne's murder. As we approach the small hotel where Jake is staying, I can't help but feel a mix of anticipation and dread.

Since he was her boyfriend, Jake obviously would've been closest to Marianne in her final days. If anyone has insight into what led to her death, it's him.

"What do you think he knows?" Charlie asks, voicing the question that's been tumbling around in my mind.

I shake my head. "I'm not sure. But he might have seen something, heard something. Maybe he knows about the blackmail note, or if Marianne was having conflicts with anyone."

As we push through the hotel's revolving door, the cool air-conditioned lobby is a sharp contrast to the heat outside. But the atmosphere inside is far from relaxed. The first thing I notice is Jake, standing near the reception desk, his posture tense and defensive. Across from him, looking equally agitated, is Samuel Goodson, Marianne's agent.

"I'm telling you, Goodson, I don't know anything about what Marianne might have had in the works, and even if I did, I wouldn't tell you!" Jake's voice carries across the lobby, drawing curious glances from the few other people milling about.

Samuel takes a step closer to Jake, his face flushed with anger. "You were her boyfriend, for God's sake! How can you not know what she was working on?"

"Maybe because unlike you, I respected her privacy," Jake spits back. "Besides, wasn't it your job to know those things? Weren't you the one who was supposed to be finding work for her—oh, that's right. No. You couldn't seem to do that, could you? That's why she was constantly trying to hustle and find bit parts to play on the side."

Charlie and I exchange a glance. The animosity between these two is palpable, crackling in the air like static electricity. We approach cautiously, and I clear my throat to announce our presence.

Both men turn to look at us. Jake's face softens slightly when he recognizes us, but Samuel's scowl only deepens.

"Lena, Charlie," Jake nods in greeting. "What brings you here?"

"We were hoping to talk to you, actually," I say, trying to keep my voice neutral. "If you have a moment?"

Jake glances at Samuel, then back to us. "Yeah, of course. Anything to get away from this snake." He jerks his thumb in Samuel's direction.

Samuel bristles. "We're not done here, Jake. This conversation isn't over."

"Yes, it is," Jake says firmly, then turns to us. "Let's go up to my room. We can talk there without any... interruptions." The look he shoots at Samuel leaves no doubt about who he considers an interruption.

As we follow Jake to the elevators, I can feel Samuel's eyes burning into our backs. There's definitely more going on here than a simple disagreement between Marianne's boyfriend and her agent. I file that observation away for later consideration as we step into the elevator.

Jake's room is on the third floor, a small, impersonal space that shows signs of extended occupancy—clothes draped over chairs, takeout containers on the desk, an open suitcase spilling its contents onto the floor. Jake clears some space on the bed for Charlie and me to sit, while he takes the desk chair.

"Sorry about the mess," he says, running a hand through his disheveled hair. "I wasn't exactly planning on an extended stay in New Oslo."

"About that," Charlie says gently. "We couldn't help but overhear... are you and Samuel both staying here?"

Jake's face darkens. "Yeah, police orders. We're not allowed to leave town until they clear us of any involvement in Marianne's..." he trails off, unable to say the word 'murder'. After a moment, he continues, "It's standard procedure, I guess, but it feels like being in prison. This town... I can't stand being here anymore. Every street, every building, it all reminds me of her."

The pain in his voice is raw and real. Whatever else is going on, it's clear that Jake is genuinely grieving for Marianne. I feel a pang of sympathy for him, trapped in this town that's become a constant reminder of his loss.

"We're sorry, Jake," I say softly. "We know this must be incredibly difficult for you. We were hoping you might be able to help us understand what happened to Marianne. Did you notice anything unusual in the days leading up to... that night?"

Jake is quiet for a long moment, his gaze fixed on a point somewhere beyond the hotel room's walls. When he finally speaks, his voice is low and thoughtful. "She was... different, those last few days. Distracted, you know? Like her mind was always somewhere else."

"Different how?" Charlie prompts gently.

Jake shrugs, frustration evident in the gesture. "It's hard to explain. She was secretive, always on her phone or her laptop. When I'd ask what she was working on, she'd just say it was research for a new part. But it felt like more than that."

"Research? Do you know what kind of research?"

"Not really," Jake admits. "She mentioned something about a show based on her hometown—New Oslo, I guess—but she was pretty vague about the details. I didn't think much of it at the time, you know? Marianne was always diving deep into research for her roles. But after what the mayor said the other night... I can't help but wonder if it was connected to what happened to her."

Charlie and I exchange a glance. Was that all there was to it? Research for a possible reality show that was never going to make it into production? Or was there something else?

"Jake," I say carefully, "did Marianne ever mention anything about being blackmailed? Or any conflicts she might have been having with someone?"

Jake's head snaps up, his eyes wide with surprise. "Blackmail? No, she never said anything about that. What are you talking about?"

I hesitate, unsure how much to reveal. But if we want Jake's help, we need to be honest with him. Briefly, I explain about the note we found in Marianne's purse.

Jake listens intently, his face growing increasingly pale. When I finish, he stands abruptly, pacing the small room. "I can't believe this," he mutters. "Why wouldn't she tell me about something like that?"

"Maybe she was trying to protect you," Charlie suggests gently.

Jake laughs, a harsh, bitter sound. "Protect me? Look where that got her." He stops pacing, turning to face us with a determined expression. "You want to know who you should really be investigating? Samuel Goodson. That man is as crooked as they come."

"What do you mean?" I ask, leaning forward.

Jake's words come out in a rush, as if he's been holding them back for days. "He's a fraud, plain and simple. Always talking about these big Hollywood connections, these amazing opportunities he was lining up for Marianne. But I never saw any evidence of it. And the jobs he did send her on? They never seemed to pan out."

"What kind of jobs?" Charlie asks, leaning forward with interest.

Jake shakes his head in frustration. "That's just it—his stories were always changing. One day he'd say Marianne was up for a big studio film, the next it was an indie project in Canada. He'd send her on these mysterious meetings, but nothing ever came of them."

"Can you give us an example?" I press, sensing there's more to this.

Jake nods, his brow furrowing as he recalls. "Okay, so about a month ago, Samuel tells Marianne he's arranged a meeting with a big-shot producer in New York. Very hush-hush, very exclusive. Marianne's excited, right? She flies out there, spends three days in the city. But when she comes back..."

"What happened?" Charlie prompts when Jake trails off.

"Nothing. Absolutely nothing," Jake says, his voice tight with anger. "She said the meeting kept getting pushed back, then canceled altogether. Samuel claimed the producer had a 'family emergency,' but I don't buy it."

I exchange a glance with Charlie. "Did Marianne seem suspicious?"

Jake sighs. "She was disappointed, sure, but she trusted Samuel. Said these things happen in the industry all the time. But then, two weeks later, Samuel's telling her about this amazing opportunity to audition for a period drama filming in England. Same story—Marianne goes, comes back empty-handed."

"And whenever I'd ask for details," Jake continues, his frustration evident, "he'd get defensive, say I was interfering with his client relationship. He'd say things like, 'This is a delicate business, Jake. One wrong move and the whole deal could fall apart.' It was always some excuse."

As Jake talks, I can feel the pieces of the puzzle shifting in my mind. Samuel's inconsistent stories, the mysterious jobs, his heated argument with Jake in the lobby—it all paints a picture of a man with something to hide.

"Jake," I say carefully, "do you think these 'jobs' might have been something else entirely? Could Samuel have been using them as a cover for... I don't know, something illegal?"

Jake's eyes widen. "I... I never thought about it like that. But now that you mention it... Marianne did say something odd after that New York trip. She joked that with all the secrecy and last-minute changes, she felt more like a spy than an actress."

"A spy?" Charlie repeats, her voice sharp. "Did she elaborate on that?"

Jake shakes his head. "I didn't think much of it at the time. But looking back... maybe there was more to it than I realized."

"Do you think Samuel could have been involved in Marianne's death?" I ask, finally voicing the question that's been hovering unspoken between us.

Jake runs a hand over his face, suddenly looking exhausted. "I don't know. I want to say no—I mean, he was Marianne's agent, he was supposed to be on her side. But the way he's been acting since it happened... it's not right. He's more concerned about damage control than finding out what really happened to her."

"What do you mean by damage control?" Charlie asks.

Jake's expression darkens. "He's been making calls non-stop, talking about 'managing the narrative' and 'protecting Marianne's image.' It's like he's more worried about how her death will affect his business than actually grieving for her or wanting justice."

I lean back, processing this new information. "Jake, this is really helpful. Thank you for being so open with us."

Jake nods, a determined look settling on his face. "I loved Marianne. If Samuel had anything to do with what happened to her... I want to know. And I want him to pay."

Before we can say anything else, he suddenly straightens up, a determined look in his eye. "You know what? I want to help you confront him."

"What?" I say, taken aback by the sudden offer.

"Samuel. His room is just down the hall from mine. Let's go talk to him right now," Jake says, his voice gaining enthusiasm. "I'd love nothing more than to see that smug jerk squirm when you confront him with the truth."

Charlie and I exchange a glance, silently debating the pros and cons of this unexpected turn of events. On one hand, having Jake with us might make Samuel more likely to talk. On the other, the obvious animosity between the two men could complicate things.

But Jake is already moving toward the door. "Come on," he says, his hand on the doorknob. "Let's go get some answers."

Chapter 9

The hallway seems to stretch endlessly as Jake leads us toward Samuel's room. The carpet muffles our footsteps, but I can hear my heart pounding in my ears. Charlie catches my eye, her expression a mix of anticipation and apprehension that I'm sure mirrors my own.

As we approach Samuel's door, Jake's posture stiffens. He raises his hand to knock, but before his knuckles can make contact, the door swings open. Samuel stands there, his tie loosened and his usually slicked-back hair slightly disheveled. The surprise on his face quickly morphs into irritation when he sees Jake.

"What do you want now?" Samuel snaps, his gaze darting between Jake, Charlie, and me. "I thought I made myself clear downstairs."

Jake opens his mouth to respond, but I step forward, hoping to diffuse the tension. "Mr. Goodson, we were hoping we could talk to you about Marianne. We have some questions that—"

"No," Samuel cuts me off abruptly. "I have nothing to say to any of you." And with that, he slams the door in our faces.

The three of us stand there in stunned silence for a moment. Then Jake's face hardens with determination. He pounds on the door. "Open up, Goodson! Unless you want me to start shouting about all your lies and fraud right here in the hallway!"

There's a pause, and for a second, I think Jake's threat has fallen on deaf ears. But then we hear the click of the lock, and the door opens once more. Samuel's face is a mask of barely contained fury.

"Get in here," he hisses, stepping aside to let us enter. "Before someone hears you."

As we file into the room, I can't help but gape at our surroundings. While Jake's accommodations were modest at best, Samuel's suite is downright luxurious. Plush carpets, a separate sitting area, even a small kitchenette—it's more like a high-end apartment than a hotel room.

Samuel closes the door behind us and turns, his arms crossed defensively over his chest. "Well? What do you want?"

"Mr. Goodson," I begin, keeping my voice as neutral as possible, "we're trying to understand the circumstances surrounding Marianne's death. We were hoping you might be able to provide some insight into her recent activities, her state of mind in the days leading up to her murder."

Samuel's laugh is harsh and humorless. "And why, pray tell, should I tell you anything? You're not the police. You're not even professionals. You're just a bunch of nosy small-town busybodies who can't mind their own business."

I feel a flash of anger at his dismissive tone, but I push it down. Getting emotional won't help us here. "Mr. Goodson," I say, my voice cooler now, "we have reason to believe that you haven't been entirely truthful about your relationship with Marianne or the nature of your business dealings."

Samuel's eyes narrow. "What are you implying?"

Charlie steps in smoothly. "We're not implying anything, Mr. Goodson. We're simply seeking the truth. If you'd prefer, we could take our concerns to Sheriff Mark. I'm sure he'd be very interested in—"

"Wait," Samuel interrupts, a flicker of panic crossing his face. He runs a hand through his hair, messing it up further. "Just...

wait a minute. Okay. Fine. You want the truth? I'll give you the truth. But I warn you, you might not like what you hear."

He moves to the minibar, pouring himself a generous measure of amber liquid. He doesn't offer us any. After taking a long swig, he turns back to face us.

"Yes, I've been involved in some... less than reputable business dealings," he admits, his voice bitter. "This industry... it's not all glitz and glamour, you know. Sometimes you have to cut corners, bend the rules a little to get ahead."

"What kind of 'corners' are we talking about here?" Jake demands, his fists clenched at his sides.

Samuel shoots him a withering look. "Nothing violent, if that's what you're implying. Some creative accounting, a few exaggerated credentials, the occasional empty promise to a wannabe starlet. It's how the game is played."

"And Marianne?" I press. "Was she part of these 'games'?"

For the first time since we entered the room, Samuel's expression softens. "No," he says quietly. "Marianne was different. She was the real deal. Talented, driven, destined for greatness. She was one of the few legitimate clients I had."

"Then why all the mysterious meetings? The constant travel? The jobs that never seemed to pan out?" Charlie asks.

Samuel sighs heavily, sinking into one of the plush armchairs. "Some of those were real opportunities. Others... well, let's just say they served a dual purpose. Marianne got to make connections, and I got to... take care of some personal business."

"Personal business," Jake repeats, his voice dripping with sarcasm. "You mean your gambling debts? Your legal troubles?"

Samuel's head snaps up, his eyes flashing with anger. "You don't know anything about my life, you sanctimonious little—"

"Enough," I interject, stepping between them before things can escalate further. "Mr. Goodson, are you saying you used Marianne's career as a cover for your own activities?"

He nods reluctantly. "Sometimes. But I swear, I never did anything to harm her career. In fact, I was on the verge of landing her biggest role yet when..." he trails off, unable to finish the sentence.

Charlie leans forward, her interest piqued. "What role was that, Mr. Goodson?"

Samuel's eyes light up for a moment. "A lead in a major studio production. It would have been her breakthrough."

"And now?" Jake asks, his tone skeptical. "Convenient that we can't verify this, isn't it?"

Samuel glares at him. "You think I'm making this up? Call Barbara Kingsly at Paramount. She'll tell you—"

"Wait," I interrupt, "You're saying Paramount was interested in Marianne? For what project?"

Samuel hesitates, then sighs. "I can't give you details. Confidentiality agreements and all that. But it was big. Really big."

Jake scoffs. "More lies. Marianne would have told me about something like that."

"Would she?" Samuel retorts. "Seems there was a lot she wasn't telling you, wasn't there, Jake?"

The tension in the room ratchets up another notch. I glance at Charlie, seeing my own unease reflected in her eyes.

"Mr. Goodson," I say gently, trying to steer the conversation back on track, "I have to ask. Did you have anything to do with Marianne's death?"

The look he gives me is one of pure anguish. "God, no," he whispers. "Marianne was... she was my ticket out of all this. My chance to go legit, to be the agent I always wanted to be. Her death... it's not just a personal tragedy. It's the end of everything I've been working towards."

"What do you mean, 'go legit'?" Charlie asks. "Weren't you already a legitimate agent?"

Samuel laughs bitterly. "Legitimate? In Hollywood? That's a relative term, sweetheart."

"Don't call her that," Jake snaps.

Samuel ignores him, continuing, "This industry... it chews you up and spits you out. Sometimes you have to cut corners just to stay afloat. But Marianne... she was different. She was my chance to do things right."

"And now?" I prompt.

He downs the rest of his drink in one gulp. "Now? Do you have any idea what I'm facing now? Legal bills, gambling debts, angry clients... Marianne was my golden goose, and now she's gone. I'm ruined."

"Anyone who could use another person like that is capable of anything," Jake mutters. "Including murder."

Samuel's eyes flash dangerously. "Watch it, boy. You're treading on thin ice."

"Is that a threat?" Jake challenges, taking a step forward.

I put a hand on Jake's arm, trying to calm him. "Jake, please. This isn't helping."

Samuel's lips curl into a sneer. "Oh, but it is helping. Because you know what? If we're talking about people with something to hide, why don't you ask lover boy here about his plans to dump Marianne?"

All eyes in the room swivel to Jake, whose face has gone pale. "W-What are you talking about?" he stammers.

Samuel's laugh is cruel. "Oh, come on. Don't play innocent. I overheard you on the phone just last week, talking about how you couldn't take it anymore, how you were going to end things after the premiere."

I turn to Jake, shock and disappointment warring inside me. "Jake? Is this true?"

For a moment, Jake looks like he might deny it. But then his shoulders slump in defeat. "It's... it's not what you think," he says quietly.

"Then what is it?" Charlie asks, her voice gentle but firm.

Jake takes a deep breath, his eyes fixed on the floor. "Yes, I was considering breaking things off with Marianne," he admits. "But not because I didn't love her. It was because... because I found out she was having an affair."

The room goes completely silent. I feel like I've been punched in the gut. Marianne, having an affair? It seems impossible, and yet...

"An affair?" I repeat, my voice barely above a whisper. "With who?"

Jake finally looks up, his eyes meeting mine. The pain I see there makes my heart ache. "With Tyler Hanson," he says. "The school teacher. Here in New Oslo."

Chapter 10

The late afternoon sun casts long shadows across Tyler Hanson's neatly manicured lawn as Charlie, Jake, and I approach his front door. I've known Tyler since high school, but today, he's not just an old classmate or a local teacher. He's a potential murderer.

I exchange a glance with Charlie. Her usually cheerful face is set in determination, mirroring my own resolve. Jake, Marianne's boyfriend—or perhaps ex-boyfriend, given recent revelations—stands slightly apart, his jaw clenched and eyes stormy.

As I raise my hand to knock, I can't help but think about how surreal this all is. Just a week ago, my biggest concern was hosting a viewing party for Marianne's new movie. Now, I'm hunting for her killer.

The door swings open before I can knock, revealing Tyler in a rumpled button-down shirt and khakis. His eyes widen slightly before he schools his expression into polite curiosity.

"Lena, Charlie," he nods, then his gaze lands on Jake. "And... Jake, right? Marianne's boyfriend? What brings you all here?"

I take a deep breath, steeling myself for the confrontation ahead. "Tyler, we need to talk about Marianne. It's important."

Tyler's eyebrows furrow, a mix of confusion and wariness crossing his face. "Marianne? What about her? I mean, I know what happened is terrible, but I'm not sure how I can help."

"Can we come in?" Charlie interjects, her tone gentle but firm. "This isn't really a conversation for the front porch."

Tyler hesitates, his eyes darting between the three of us. "I... I suppose so. Though I'm not sure what you think I can tell you that the police don't already know."

Jake, who's been uncharacteristically quiet, speaks up. "Trust me, Tyler. You'll want to have this conversation inside."

Tyler's face pales slightly at Jake's tone, but he nods, stepping back to allow us entry. "Alright, come on in. But I really don't know what this is about."

We follow Tyler into his living room, a cozy space filled with bookshelves and framed family photos. As we settle onto the worn leather couch, I can't help but notice how Tyler positions himself near the window, occasionally glancing outside as if keeping watch.

"So," Tyler begins, his voice carefully neutral, "what about Marianne did you want to discuss? I've already given my statement to the police."

I lean forward, my eyes locked on Tyler's face. "We know you and Marianne had a... complicated relationship. We need to understand what was going on between you two."

Tyler's expression hardens, his posture becoming defensive. "I don't know what you're talking about. Marianne and I were old classmates, nothing more. Whatever you think you know—"

"Cut the act, Tyler," Jake interrupts, his voice low and intense. "We're not here to play games. We know there was more between you and Marianne than just being 'old classmates.'"

Tyler's eyes widen, and he glances nervously towards the window again. "Keep your voice down," he hisses. "My neighbors... they're nosy. Look, I don't know what you think you know, but you're mistaken. Marianne and I were friends, that's all."

Charlie leans in, her voice gentle but persistent. "Tyler, we're not here to judge. We just want to understand what happened. If you and Marianne were just friends, why do you keep looking out the window? Why are you so worried about being overheard?"

Tyler fidgets and looks back and forth between the three of us, clearly agitated. "You don't understand. This is a small town. People talk. I'm a teacher, for goodness sake. I can't have rumors spreading about me and Marianne. It would ruin me."

"Rumors?" I press, sensing we're close to a breakthrough. "What kind of rumors, Tyler? What are you afraid people might say?"

Tyler's face contorts, a mix of fear and frustration. "Nothing! There's nothing to say because nothing happened. Why can't you just leave it alone?"

"Because Marianne is dead," Jake says bluntly, his voice cracking slightly on the last word. "And we need to know the truth to find out who killed her."

The room falls silent for a moment, the weight of Jake's words hanging heavy in the air. Tyler's face pales, and he sinks into the armchair across from us, the fight seeming to drain out of him.

"Look," Jake continues, his voice low and intense, "I didn't want to believe it at first. But I saw the text messages between you and Marianne. You were threatening her, Tyler. Don't try to deny it."

His head snaps up, his eyes wide with shock. "You... you saw the messages? How? Marianne wouldn't... she promised she'd deleted them."

"She didn't," Jake says, his voice tight with barely contained anger. "I found them the night before... before she died. I was going to confront her about it, but then..."

He trails off, unable to finish the sentence. The pain in his voice is palpable, and I resist the urge to reach out and comfort him. Instead, I focus on Tyler, whose facade of innocence has completely crumbled.

"Tyler," I say gently, "this is your chance to tell us the truth. What really happened between you and Marianne?"

He buries his face in his hands for a moment, then looks up at us, his eyes filled with a mixture of shame and resignation. "I... I didn't mean to threaten her," he says softly. "It was a moment of weakness, of anger. I regretted it immediately."

"Start from the beginning," Charlie urges, her voice calm and reassuring. "Tell us everything. It's the only way we can get to the bottom of this."

He nods slowly, taking a deep breath. "Okay," he says, his voice barely above a whisper. "Okay, I'll tell you everything. But you have to understand, I never wanted to hurt Marianne. I loved her, in my own way."

"Marianne and I... we had a history," he begins, his voice shaky. "We dated in high school, before she left for Hollywood. When she called and told me she was making a movie about New Oslo, all those old feelings resurfaced. It was like no time had passed at all."

He pauses, glancing at the family photos on the mantel. His gaze lingers on a picture of a smiling woman—his wife, I assume—and a young child. The pain in his eyes is palpable.

"At first, it was just coffee, catching up," Tyler continues. "But then it became more. We started texting all the time. For a while, I thought... I thought maybe we could rekindle something."

"But you're married," I prompt gently, when Tyler falls silent.

He nods, his face a mask of guilt. "Yes. I'm married. I have a family. And when it came down to it, I couldn't bear the thought of betraying my wife like that. But I'd be lying if I said I didn't still have feelings for Marianne. I probably always will."

"So what happened?" Charlie asks. "If you decided not to pursue a relationship with Marianne, why the threatening texts?"

Tyler's face contorts with shame. "It was stupid. I was angry, hurt. When I realized nothing was going to happen between us and she kept pushing for more, I... I lashed out."

"Lashed out how?" Jake demands, his voice hard.

Tyler flinches at Jake's tone but continues. "I threatened to tell everyone about our almos—affair. To expose her to the tabloids if she didn't... if she didn't pay me off."

The room falls silent as we process this information. Jake stands abruptly, his fists clenched at his sides. "You tried to blackmail her? You son of a—"

"Jake," I interrupt, placing a calming hand on his arm. "Let him finish."

Tyler nods gratefully, then continues. "I know how it sounds. I'm not proud of it. It was a moment of madness, and I regretted it almost immediately."

"So what happened then?" I press. "Did Marianne pay you off?"

Tyler shakes his head vehemently. "No, no. She refused, of course. She was furious, and she had every right to be. But then... then she was understanding. Too understanding, really."

"What do you mean?" Charlie asks, leaning forward.

"She forgave me," Tyler says, his voice filled with wonder and regret. "Can you believe that? After what I'd done, she forgave me. Said she understood that I was hurting, that she was sorry for letting things get out of hand. I didn't deserve her forgiveness."

"But you took it," Jake says bitterly.

Tyler nods, unable to meet Jake's eyes. "I did. We talked it out, agreed to put it all behind us. To just be friends, like we should have been from the start."

"And that was it?" I ask, sensing there's more to the story. "You just went back to being friends?"

Tyler hesitates, and I can see the internal struggle playing out on his face. "Not... not exactly," he admits finally. "There's something else you should know."

He stands suddenly, startling us. "Wait here," he says, disappearing down the hallway. We exchange confused glances, wondering what else this troubled man could possibly reveal.

When he returns, he's holding something in his hand—a delicate gold necklace with a pendant. My breath catches in my throat as I recognize it. It's the same necklace Marianne was wearing the night she died.

"I bought this for her," Tyler explains, his voice thick with emotion. "After we agreed to just be friends. It was my way of acknowledging our feelings for each other, but also putting a stop to any talk of a relationship."

The necklace dangles between us, catching the late afternoon light. It's beautiful, delicate—and potentially damning evidence. I can't take my eyes off it, my mind racing with the implications of its presence here in Tyler's house.

"When I saw her wearing it at the premiere," Tyler continues, "I didn't know whether to feel upset or happy. Part of me was glad she'd accepted it, that she understood what it meant. But another part..."

"Another part what?" Jake prompts, his voice tight with barely contained emotion.

Tyler sighs heavily. "Another part of me was jealous, I suppose. Seeing her there, so beautiful, so successful. Wearing my necklace, but on your arm. It brought up a lot of complicated feelings."

"Tyler," Charlie says softly, her voice filled with dawning realization, "how did you get that necklace? It was on Marianne when she..." She trails off, unable to finish the sentence.

His face crumples, and for a moment, I think he might break down completely. When he speaks, his voice is barely audible. "After... after what happened, I couldn't leave it on her. I was afraid my wife might find out."

The implications of his words hit me like a physical blow. Tyler had touched her body, removed evidence from the crime scene. The necklace dangles between us, a tangible link to the night of the murder.

"I was as shocked as everyone else when I saw that she'd been killed," he says. "And then, when I realized... when I saw her like that... I panicked. All I could think about was the necklace, what it would mean if anyone found out about it."

"So you just took it?" Jake demands, his voice rising with anger. "You saw her lying there, murdered, and all you cared about was covering your own mess?"

"It wasn't like that!" Tyler protests, tears welling in his eyes. "I was in shock. I wasn't thinking straight. I know it was wrong, I know I should have told the police everything right away. But I was scared."

"Scared of what, exactly?" Charlie asks, her tone gentler than Jake's but no less probing.

Tyler gestures helplessly around the room, at the family photos, the signs of a comfortable, settled life. "Of losing all this. My job, my family, my reputation. If people found out about my history with Marianne, about the blackmail... I thought my life would be over."

"So you lied," I say, not a question but a statement.

Tyler nods, shame written across his features. "I lied. To the police, to you, to everyone. I thought if I just pretended nothing had happened between Marianne and me, it would all go away. But I swear to you, I didn't kill her. I loved her, in my own way. I could never have hurt her like that."

I watch Tyler carefully, trying to gauge his sincerity. His remorse seems genuine, but can I trust it? After all, he's already admitted to lying once. How can we be sure he's telling the truth now?

"Tyler," I say slowly, my mind racing, "you do realize how this looks, don't you? You've just admitted to having a motive—multiple motives, in fact—for wanting Marianne dead. The blackmail attempt, the affair, removing evidence from the crime scene... It doesn't paint a good picture."

He nods, his face a mask of resignation. "I know. I understand how bad this looks. But I swear to you, I'm not a murderer. I made mistakes, terrible mistakes, but I didn't kill Marianne."

"Intent isn't always necessary for a murder charge," Charlie points out gently. "You were there that night with plenty of reasons to have Marianne out of the way..."

"No!" Tyler exclaims, his voice cracking. "No, it wasn't like that. I told you, I never would've hurt her. Never wanted to."

Jake, who has been pacing the room restlessly, stops to face Tyler. "And we're just supposed to take your word for that? After you've lied about everything else?"

Tyler slumps in his chair, looking utterly defeated. "I don't know what else to say. I've told you everything now. I know it's not enough, but it's the truth. I swear it."

I stand, feeling the weight of responsibility settle on my shoulders. "I believe that you believe that, Tyler. But I'm going to have to give this information to Sheriff Mark. You understand that, right?"

He meets my gaze, his eyes filled with a mixture of fear and acceptance. "I understand. Do what you have to do, Lena. I just... I hope the truth comes out. For Marianne's sake, if nothing else."

"Is there anything else?" Charlie asks, her voice gentle but probing. "Anything at all that might help us understand what happened that night?"

Tyler shakes his head slowly. "I've told you everything I know. I... I'm sorry. For lying, for everything. I never meant for any of this to happen."

As we leave Tyler's house, the sun has dipped below the horizon, casting long shadows across the quiet street. The necklace is secure in an evidence bag in my purse, its weight a reminder of the tangled web of relationships and secrets we've uncovered.

Charlie squeezes my arm reassuringly. "What now?" she asks.

I take a deep breath, my mind already racing ahead to our next steps. "Now, we talk to Sheriff Mark."

Chapter 11

The fluorescent lights of the New Oslo Police Station flicker overhead as Charlie, Jake, and I push through the heavy glass doors. The dispatcher looks up from her desk, her eyebrows rising in recognition.

"Lena," she says, a hint of amusement in her voice, "I swear, you're here more often than some of our deputies. Sheriff Mark's expecting you."

I nod, trying to muster a smile but failing. The weight of Tyler's confession and the necklace safely tucked away in my purse feel like anchors dragging me down. Charlie squeezes my arm reassuringly as we make our way down the corridor to Mark's office.

Jake trails behind us, uncharacteristically quiet. I can't help but wonder what's going through his mind. How is he processing all of this? Finding out about Marianne's almost— affair with Tyler, the blackmail attempt, the lies... it's a lot for anyone to handle, let alone the person who loved her most.

As we approach Mark's office, I catch a glimpse of our reflections in the glass panels lining the hallway. We look exhausted, disheveled—a far cry from the excited group that gathered for Marianne's viewing party just a few days ago. It's amazing how quickly life can change, how a single moment can shatter everything you thought you knew.

I raise my hand to knock on Mark's door, but before my knuckles can make contact, his gruff voice calls out, "Come on in, Lena. Door's open."

Taking a deep breath, I push the door open, ushering Charlie and Jake in before me. Mark's office is cluttered but cozy, stacks of case files competing for space with photos and the odd knick-knack.

"Well," he says, gesturing for us to take a seat, "I hear you've had quite the eventful afternoon. Why don't you fill me in on what you've discovered?"

I don't waste any time launching into everything we've learned. As I finish recounting our conversation with Tyler, laying out the tangled web of past relationships, blackmail attempts, and incriminating evidence, Sheriff Mark lets out a low whistle. He leans back in his chair, the old wood creaking in protest, and fixes me with a look that's equal parts impressed and exasperated.

"Congratulations, Lena," he says, shaking his head slightly. "I swear, I don't know how you manage to keep solving these mysteries, but I do appreciate the help. It looks like you've brought another murderer to justice."

I shift uncomfortably in my seat, the praise sitting uneasily on my shoulders. "I'm not sure I'd go that far, Mark," I begin, but he waves off my protest.

"Don't be modest," he insists. "You've done it again. As much as I'd like to keep you out of harm's way, I have to admit you've got a real knack for this detective work."

Charlie beams proudly beside me, but I can't bring myself to share in the enthusiasm. Something about this doesn't feel right, doesn't feel finished.

Mark continues, seemingly oblivious to my discomfort. "I'll send a couple of deputies over to Tyler's place right away. We'll bring him in for formal questioning, get a full confession. With the evidence you've gathered—the necklace, the blackmail, and the rest—we should be able to wrap this up pretty quickly."

"But—" I start to interject, only to be cut off again.

"I know, I know," Mark says, holding up a hand. "You're probably thinking about the trial, the legal proceedings. But take a minute to pat yourself on the back. This is good work, Lena. You should be proud."

I glance at Jake, who's been silent throughout the entire exchange. His face is a mask of conflicting emotions—relief, anger, confusion, and something else I can't quite place. Does he believe Tyler is guilty? Does he want to?

"Sheriff," Jake speaks up suddenly, his voice rough. "What happens now? To Tyler, I mean."

Mark's expression softens slightly. "Well, once we bring him in and get his official statement, he'll be formally charged. There'll be an arraignment, bail hearing... but given the nature of the crime, I'd expect him to remain in custody until trial."

Jake nods, his jaw clenching. I can see the struggle playing out on his face—the desire for justice warring with the shock of everything he's learned about Marianne in the past few hours.

As I watch Jake grapple with these emotions, as I see the satisfaction on Mark's face and the pride on Charlie's, I know I can't let this stand. Not yet. Not when there are still so many unanswered questions swirling in my mind.

"Wait," I say, my voice firmer than I expected. "Mark, I appreciate the praise, but I'm not sure we've solved anything yet. Something about this still doesn't add up."

Mark's eyebrows furrow, and he leans forward, elbows on his desk. "What do you mean? We've got motive, opportunity, and physical evidence. What more do you need?"

I take a deep breath, organizing my thoughts. How can I explain this nagging feeling, this sense that we're missing something crucial? "I know it looks bad for Tyler," I begin slowly. "The affair, the blackmail attempt, him being at the scene... it all points to him. But something feels off."

Charlie turns to me, surprise evident on her face. "Lena, are you saying you don't think Tyler did it? After everything he confessed to us?"

I shake my head, frustrated at my inability to articulate my doubts clearly. "I'm not saying that exactly. I'm saying... I'm saying we might be jumping to conclusions. There are still pieces of this puzzle that don't fit."

Mark sighs, running a hand through his thinning hair. "Lena, I know you have good instincts. They've certainly helped solve cases before. But sometimes the simplest explanation is the right one. Tyler had motive, opportunity, and he's admitted to being at the scene. What more do you need?"

"Evidence that actually ties him to the murder," I counter. "Yes, he was there, but so were the rest of us. Yes, he had motive, but so did others."

Jake, who's been quiet until now, speaks up. "She's right," he says softly. "As much as I want... as much as I thought I wanted to have someone to blame, to punish... we can't ignore other possibilities."

Mark looks between us, his expression a mix of confusion and growing frustration. "Okay," he says finally. "What exactly are you suggesting? What 'pieces' don't fit for you, Lena?"

I lean forward, grateful for the chance to explain. "It's not just one thing, Mark. It's a combination of little details that don't quite add up. The timeline feels off. The way Tyler describes his interactions with Marianne doesn't match with a premeditated murder. And then there's the physical evidence..."

"Such as?"

"The knife," I say, my voice growing more confident as I lay out my concerns. "The murder weapon. We still haven't addressed the fingerprints found on it."

Mark's brow furrows deeper. "That's right. I'd almost forgotten they didn't match anyone at the party. We assumed they might belong to someone who handled the knife before that night—maybe someone from the catering staff or one of the workers who set up for the event."

I shake my head, leaning forward in my chair. "That's just it, Mark. Don't you think that's odd? If Tyler killed Marianne in a fit of passion or anger, wouldn't his prints be on the knife? And if he was cold and calculating enough to wipe the knife clean, why leave it at the scene at all, especially when he went to all the risk and trouble to grab the necklace she was wearing?"

Charlie nods slowly beside me, catching on to my train of thought. "She's right, Sheriff. It doesn't make sense. Either Tyler was careful enough to clean the knife, in which case why not dispose of it entirely, or he wasn't thinking clearly and acted on impulse, in which case his prints should be there."

Mark leans back in his chair. "Okay, I see your point about the knife. It is strange. But strange doesn't necessarily mean Tyler isn't guilty. Maybe he wore gloves. Maybe someone else picked up the knife afterward, contaminating the evidence."

I nod, acknowledging the possibility. "You're right, it doesn't rule Tyler out completely. But it does suggest we might be missing something. I believe Tyler did a lot of stupid, questionable things. The affair, the blackmail attempt, taking the necklace from the scene—those are all terrible decisions that he'll have to face consequences for. But... I don't think he killed Marianne."

The room falls silent for a moment as everyone processes my words. I can see the conflict playing out on their faces—the desire for a neat resolution warring with the nagging doubts I've brought to light.

Jake is the first to speak. "I... I think I agree with Lena," he says, his voice rough with emotion. "As much as I want someone to blame, it doesn't feel right. Tyler's actions were despicable, but murder? I'm not so sure."

Charlie nods slowly. "When we were talking to Tyler, his remorse seemed genuine. He was scared, yes, and he made some horrific choices, but he didn't strike me as a killer."

Mark leans back in his chair, his expression thoughtful. "Alright, let's say for a moment that you're right. That Tyler isn't our killer. Where does that leave us? We're back to square one, with a murderer still on the loose."

"I know," I acknowledge. "And I'm not asking you to let him off the hook. But maybe... maybe we hold off on formally charging him with murder until we've explored some other avenues?"

Mark leans forward, clasping his hands on his desk. "Okay, let's think this through. If Tyler isn't our killer, what does that mean for the investigation? What are we missing?"

I consider for a moment before responding. "It means we need to look at everything with fresh eyes. We've been so focused on Tyler that we might have overlooked crucial details about our other suspects."

Jake speaks up, his voice quiet but determined. "I want to help. Whatever you need—interviews, research, anything. I need to know the truth about what happened to Marianne."

I reach out and squeeze his hand, touched by his willingness to push through his pain to find justice. "We'll figure this out, Jake. Together."

As we leave Mark's office, I feel a renewed sense of purpose. The case isn't solved—far from it. But now, at least, we're asking the right questions.

Chapter 12

A loud clatter jolts me awake. My eyes snap open, heart racing. The room is dark, moonlight barely seeping through the curtains. I glance at the clock: 3:17 AM.

I hold my breath, listening. The house creaks, settling. But something feels off. That noise wasn't just the old Victorian playing tricks. It was too loud, too close.

I push myself up on my elbows, squinting into the darkness. Everything looks normal—the dresser, the bookshelf, the chair with yesterday's clothes. But the air feels thick, heavy with an unseen presence.

"Who's there?" I whisper, immediately feeling foolish. If it's an intruder, they're hardly going to answer, "Oh, just me, your friendly neighborhood burglar."

The floorboards groan near the foot of my bed. I freeze, straining my eyes in the dim light. Was that a shadow moving?

"Lena, dear, now might be a good time to consider installing that security system Sheriff Mark has been nagging you about," Granny Ingrid's ghostly voice pipes up, startling me so badly I nearly fall out of bed.

"Not now, Granny," I hiss through clenched teeth. The last thing I need is a lecture on home security from my spectral grandmother.

I'm about to lie back down, convince myself it's all in my head, when I catch it—a flicker of movement in the corner of my eye. My breath hitches. I'm not alone.

The realization sends a chill down my spine. Someone's in my room, creeping around in the dark. My mind races through possibilities. A burglar? One of Marianne's enemies? Or something worse?

I reach for my phone on the nightstand, moving as slowly and quietly as I can. If I can just call for help...

My fingers brush against empty wood. The phone's not there. Panic starts to rise in my chest. Where is it? Did I leave it downstairs?

"Looking for this?" Granny's voice again, tinged with amusement. I look up to see her pointing at my desk, where my phone sits plugged into its charger. On the other side of the room. Past the moving shadow.

Great. Just great.

I sit up slowly, eyes fixed on the foot of my bed. A shadow moves there, creeping quietly. It's hunched, careful not to make noise. My mind races. Who is it? How did they get in?

"Oh, for heaven's sake, Lena," Granny Ingrid materializes beside me, her ghostly form shimmering in the darkness. "This is no time for twenty questions. Run!"

The shadow straightens, reacting to my movement. Moonlight glints off something in their hand. My blood runs cold. A knife.

"You see? This is exactly why I always told you to keep a baseball bat by your bed," Granny continues, apparently oblivious to the gravity of the situation. "But did you listen? No, of course not. 'I don't even like baseball, Granny,' you said. Well, I bet you're wishing you had one now, aren't you?"

I resist the urge to roll my eyes. Trust Granny to pick now for an I-told-you-so moment.

The intruder takes a step closer, the knife gleaming ominously. My heart pounds so hard I'm sure they must hear it.

"Lena, move!" Granny's voice cuts through my panic. "Unless you're planning on inviting them for a nice cup of tea, in which case, I must say your hospitality is getting a bit out of hand."

The door seems miles away, but it's my only chance. I take a deep breath. It's now or never.

"That's it, dear," Granny encourages. "Channel your inner track star. I always said you had the legs for it."

I gather my muscles, ready to spring. The intruder seems to sense my intention, tensing for action.

For a moment, we're locked in a standoff. Me, the ghostly peanut gallery of my grandmother, and a knife-wielding shadow in my bedroom. If I survive this, it'll make one hell of a story for my next book.

Then, like a starter pistol going off, Granny shouts, "Go, go, go!" And I launch myself into action.

The attacker lunges. Moonlight flashes on the blade. I throw myself sideways, feeling the whoosh of the near-miss. I hit the floor hard, scramble to my feet, and dash for the door.

"Ole!" Granny cheers. "Just like a matador. Though I doubt this bull will be impressed by your red pajamas."

My bare feet slap against the wood. The door's so close. My hand reaches for the knob.

Suddenly, fingers clamp around my ankle. I crash down, chin smacking the floor. Pain explodes in my jaw.

"Oh, fumble on the one-yard line," Granny groans. "Come on, Lena, this is no time for graceful floor routines!"

I kick out wildly, feeling my heel connect. A grunt of pain, but the grip doesn't loosen. Instead, I'm dragged backward.

Panic rises in my throat as I claw at the smooth floor. No use. I flip over, facing my attacker. The knife glints above me.

"Use the lamp!" Granny shouts. "The vase! The... oh, for Pete's sake, use anything!"

Fear turns to determination. I've faced worse. I'm not dying here, not tonight.

"That's my girl," Granny says proudly. "Show them what happens when people don't knock first in this house!"

I grab the nearest object—a hardcover book from my nightstand—and swing it with all my might. It connects with a satisfying thud.

The attacker reels back, momentarily stunned. I scramble to my feet, heart pounding.

"Ha! Take that!" Granny crows. "I always said reading would save your life one day."

I dash for the door again, praying I can make it this time. But I can hear the attacker recovering behind me. It's going to be close.

We collide again, rolling across the floor. The knife is between us, deadly and cold. But as we grapple, I realize something—my attacker isn't very strong. Their movements are clumsy, almost afraid.

"Well, isn't this cozy," Granny comments dryly. "I hope you're not planning on making this a regular Monday night activity, dear."

Hope surges through me. I might have a chance.

I pin them down, grabbing their wrist. I slam it against the floor, again and again. They grunt but don't let go.

"That's it, Lena! Pretend it's that jar of pickles you could never open!"

We're locked in a silent battle. Sweat drips down my face. My muscles scream. But I won't give up.

"You know," Granny muses, "this reminds me of the time your grandfather and I tried to take down the Christmas tree in '62. It was a real Douglas fir, you see, and—"

"Not now, Granny!" I grit out, still struggling with the attacker.

Finally, their grip loosens. The knife clatters to the floor. I snatch it up and scramble back.

"Ha! Disarmed!" Granny cheers. "Now that's what I call cutting-edge home defense!"

I point the knife at them, hand shaking but grip firm. They freeze, chest heaving.

For the first time, I really look at my attacker. They're smaller than I thought, almost familiar in their movements.

"Don't move," I say, surprised by how steady I sound. "It's over."

They raise their hands in surrender. But something nags at me. That posture, the way they hold themselves...

A crazy thought forms. Could it be?

I stand slowly, knife pointed at the attacker. They stay down, tense like a coiled spring.

"Take off the mask," I order. They don't move. "Now. Or I'll do it for you."

Chapter 13

"Diana Peterson?" I gasp, my voice barely above a whisper.

The face staring back at me is unmistakable—the kind eyes that are normally kind and unassuming now wide with fear, the usually perfectly coiffed hair a mess, the familiar features contorted with a mix of shame and desperation. It's my next-door neighbor, James's mother, Harold's widow.

"Well, I'll be," Granny's ghost mutters beside me. "And here I thought the most exciting thing about her was her award-winning petunia garden."

I shake my head, trying to make sense of this bizarre turn of events. Diana Peterson, in my bedroom, in the middle of the night, wielding a knife. It's like I've stepped into some twisted alternate reality where kindly neighborhood ladies moonlight as assassins.

"Mrs. Peterson," I say, struggling to keep my voice steady, "what on earth are you doing?"

She doesn't answer, her eyes darting around the room like a cornered animal. The knife in my hand suddenly feels heavier, a stark reminder of what almost happened.

The absurdity of the situation hits me all at once. Here I am, standing in my pajamas, holding a kitchen knife on a woman who, just last week, waved at me from her front porch and complimented my rose bushes.

"I have to say," I continue, a hysterical laugh bubbling up in my throat, "this is taking the whole 'borrowing a cup of sugar from your neighbor' thing to a whole new level."

The shock starts to wear off, replaced by a burning need for answers. I tighten my grip on the knife, not lowering it for a second. I may be confused, but I'm not stupid.

"Start talking, Mrs. Peterson," I demand, surprised by the steel in my voice. "Why are you in my house? Why were you trying to kill me?"

Diana flinches at my words, her face crumpling. "I... I wasn't... I didn't want to..." she stammers, each word seeming to cost her a great effort.

"Oh, of course not," I snap, my patience wearing thin. "You just thought you'd pop in for a late-night chat with a carving knife. Totally normal neighbor behavior."

"Lena," Granny's voice warns softly, "careful. There's more here than meets the eye."

I take a deep breath, trying to rein in my anger and fear. Granny's right. I need answers, not sarcasm.

"Mrs. Peterson," I try again, gentler this time. "Please. I need to understand what's happening here. Why did you break into my house? What were you planning to do?"

Diana's eyes fill with tears. She looks so lost, so unlike the confident, put-together woman I thought I knew. It's hard to reconcile this trembling figure with the person who organized our neighborhood watch and baked cookies for every new family on the block.

"I... I was trying to protect him," she whispers, her voice barely audible.

"Protect who?" I press, though a sinking feeling in my gut tells me I already know the answer.

"James," Diana chokes out, a sob escaping her. "I was trying to protect my son."

The pieces start falling into place, a picture forming that I desperately wish I could unsee. "James?" I repeat, my mind reeling. "What does James have to do with this?"

Diana looks up at me, her eyes pleading. "He... he killed her. Marianne. It was James."

"Oh, dear," Granny's voice floats in the background. "I always said that boy was too quiet. It's the quiet ones you have to watch out for."

I ignore her, focusing on Diana. "Are you saying... But why? How?"

Diana's words come out in a rush, as if now that she's started, she can't stop. "He was there that night, at your party. Ever since Harold died, James has been... different. Bitter. Angry. He wanted to find a way to get back at you for... for what he thought you did to our family."

My mind is spinning, trying to process this information.

"So James killed Marianne to somehow get back at me?" I ask, still unable to connect the dots. "But that doesn't make sense. Why frame me? Why make it look like I did it?"

Diana shakes her head, fresh tears spilling down her cheeks. "He hasn't been thinking clearly. All he could think about was protecting his father's memory, protecting our family. I love him more than anything in the world, but something snapped inside him when Harold was killed"

"And he thought he'd get his revenge at my party. By framing me."

"He never meant for it to go this far," Diana pleads. "He didn't think it through. When he realized what he'd done, he was terrified. And then you started investigating, getting closer to the truth..."

I remember the suspicious conversation Charlie and I overheard between James and Diana about "loose ends." It all makes a horrible kind of sense now.

"So you decided to take matters into your own hands," I conclude, gesturing with the knife. "Silence me before I could uncover the truth."

Diana nods miserably. "I couldn't let him go to jail. He's all I have left. I thought... I thought if I could just scare you off the case..."

"Scare me off?" I repeat incredulously. "With a knife in the middle of the night? That's not scaring someone off, Mrs. Peterson. That's attempted murder."

As Diana's words sink in, I glance down at the knife in my hand. Really look at it for the first time. The weight, the design, the worn handle—it's familiar. Too familiar.

"This knife," I say slowly, a chill running down my spine. "It matches the murder weapon, doesn't it? Because it's from the same set."

Diana nods, unable to meet my eyes. "From my kitchen," she confirms softly. "James... he took one that night. I didn't realize until later."

Suddenly, another piece of the puzzle clicks into place. "The fingerprints," I breathe. "The unidentified fingerprints on the murder weapon. They were yours, weren't they?"

"Yes," Diana whispers. "I... I handled the knives earlier that day while preparing some food. When I heard you were closing in on the killer, I... I thought I needed to do something to protect my son."

I shake my head, still struggling to process it all. "So you broke into my house, with another knife from the same set, thinking... what? That you'd stage some kind of attack? Make it look like the real killer was still out there?"

Diana nods miserably. "I didn't think it through. I just knew I had to do something, anything, to throw you off the scent. To keep James safe."

"Well," Granny's dry voice cuts in, "I'd say that plan went about as well as using a chocolate teapot."

My hand shakes as I reach for my phone, but my voice is steady as I dial Sheriff Mark's number. Diana doesn't move, doesn't try to stop me. She just sits there, defeated, as I relay the bare bones of what's happened.

Within minutes, the quiet night is shattered by the wail of sirens. Flashing lights paint my bedroom walls in surreal shades of red and blue. I hear car doors slamming, voices calling out.

"Lena?" Sheriff Mark's voice carries up the stairs. "You okay up there?"

"We're fine," I call back, not taking my eyes off Diana. "We're coming down."

I gesture for Diana to stand, keeping a safe distance between us as we make our way downstairs. The house is suddenly full of deputies, their faces a mix of concern and confusion as they take in the scene—me in my pajamas, wielding a kitchen knife, escorting my neighbor down the stairs.

As we reach the bottom, I see James being led in through the front door. Our eyes meet, and in that moment, I see the truth of everything Diana told me reflected in his gaze.

"I'm sorry, Lena," he whispers as a deputy cuffs his hands behind his back. "I never meant for any of this to happen."

I watch in silence as mother and son are read their rights, as they're led out to waiting patrol cars. The knife is bagged as evidence, statements are taken, and through it all, I feel like I'm watching from a distance, like this is happening to someone else.

As the last of the deputies file out, promising to return in the morning for a more detailed statement, Sheriff Mark turns to me. "You okay, Lena? That was a heck of a thing you just went through."

I nod, not trusting my voice just yet. How do you put into words the feeling of having your world turned upside down, of discovering that people you thought you knew were capable of murder and deceit?

"Well," Granny's voice pipes up, audible only to me, "I'd say this calls for a stiff drink and a new deadbolt. Not necessarily in that order."

For once, I find myself agreeing wholeheartedly with my spectral grandmother. As I close and lock the door behind Sheriff Mark, I lean against it, letting out a long, shaky breath.

Chapter 14

The soft glow of candlelight flickers across Mark's face as he reaches for his wine glass. I can't help but smile, marveling at how normal this feels after everything we've been through.

It's been three weeks since the night Diana Peterson broke into my house, three weeks since the truth about Marianne's murder came to light. The dust has finally started to settle, and here we are, sharing a quiet dinner in my dining room.

"This pot roast is delicious, Lena," Mark says, breaking the comfortable silence. "I had no idea you were such a good cook."

I laugh, shaking my head. "Don't get too excited. This is pretty much the extent of my culinary skills. It's either this or takeout."

He grins, his eyes crinkling at the corners in a way that makes my heart skip a beat. "Well, I'm impressed nonetheless. Though I have to admit, I'm a little surprised you're not sick of this dining room by now."

I glance around, taking in the familiar surroundings. This room has seen so much in recent weeks—late-night strategy sessions, tense interviews, moments of breakthrough and despair. Oh, and a couple of murders.

But tonight, it feels different. Softer. Warmer.

"Actually," I say, surprised to find I mean it, "I think I like it even more now. It's like... I don't know, like we've reclaimed it, you know?"

Mark nods, reaching across the table to take my hand. "I do know. And I'm glad we're here, making new memories in this space."

"You know, I can't remember the last time I had an evening this quiet. No mysteries to solve, no lives in danger, just... peace."

Mark chuckles, raising an eyebrow. "It is a nice change of pace, isn't it? Though I have to admit, part of me keeps expecting another crisis to pop up."

I laugh, understanding the feeling all too well. "Don't jinx it," I warn playfully. "I'm quite enjoying this break from the chaos."

"Me too," Mark agrees, his expression softening. "After everything that's happened... it's nice to just be here, with you, without any pressure or danger looming over us."

I nod, feeling a warmth spread through my chest at his words. The past few weeks have been a whirlwind of statements, paperwork, and court appearances. The whole town is still reeling from the revelations about James and Diana Peterson.

"It's more than nice," I admit. "It's... necessary, I think. To remind ourselves that life goes on, that there's still good in the world."

Mark squeezes my hand. "You're right. And speaking of good things, I have to say, you look beautiful tonight, Lena."

I feel a blush creeping up my cheeks. "You clean up pretty well yourself, Sheriff," I tease, trying to lighten the mood.

As we finish our meal, neither of us seems in a hurry to move. The candles have burned lower, casting long shadows across the table. Outside, the world continues its usual bustle, but in here, time seems to have slowed to a delicious crawl.

"You know," Mark says, leaning back in his chair, "I could get used to this. Quiet evenings, good food, excellent company... makes me want to just stay right here for a while."

I smile, feeling a warmth that has nothing to do with the wine. "Oh yeah? How long were you thinking? A few more hours? Days?"

He pretends to consider it seriously. "Well, let's see. We've got a lot of lost time to make up for, what with all the crime-solving and near-death experiences. I'd say... a few weeks, at least. Maybe months."

I laugh, but there's a part of me that thrills at the idea. "Months, huh? What about your job? The town's crime rate would skyrocket without Sheriff Mark on duty."

He shrugs, a mischievous glint in his eye. "We've got deputies. Besides, I think I've earned some time off, don't you? We both have."

"Can't argue with that," I admit. The idea of shutting out the world, even for a little while, is incredibly tempting. "Though I'm not sure how we'd occupy ourselves for months on end, trapped within these four walls."

Mark's grin turns decidedly wicked. "Oh, I'm sure we could think of a few things."

Just as I'm about to respond to Mark's suggestive comment, a familiar shimmer appears in my peripheral vision. I suppress a groan as Granny Ingrid materializes near the china cabinet.

"Well, well, well," she says, eyeing Mark appreciatively. "I'd almost forgotten how nicely the sheriff cleans up."

"So, Lena," Mark says, reaching for his wine glass, "I know we were sort of joking, but I really have been thinking about taking some time off. Maybe we could plan a little getaway?"

I nod, trying to focus on Mark while Granny circles the table, peering at our half-empty plates.

"Ooh, a romantic getaway," Granny coos. "How exciting! Just make sure you pack something nice, dear. Those ratty old pajamas you love so much are not appropriate vacation wear."

I barely manage to turn my snort of laughter into a cough. Mark looks at me, concerned.

"You okay?" he asks.

"Fine," I assure him, shooting a quick glare at Granny that Mark can't see. "Just went down the wrong pipe. But yes, a getaway sounds wonderful. Where were you thinking?"

Mark reaches out, gently tucking a strand of hair behind my ear. "Anywhere as long as it's with you," he says softly, his voice low and warm. "I can't tell you how glad I am that we're here, together, after everything that's happened."

I lean into his touch, my heart racing. "Me too," I whisper.

He leans in closer, his intention clear. My eyes start to flutter closed...

"Oh my!" Granny's voice rings out. "Things are certainly heating up in here. Should I leave? Or stay and take notes? It's been a while since I've seen any action, you know."

My eyes snap open, and I can't help but pull back slightly, shooting a quick glare in Granny's direction. Mark, oblivious to Granny's presence, looks confused by my reaction.

"Everything okay?" he asks, concern evident in his voice.

I nod, trying to regain the moment. "Everything's perfect," I assure him, mentally willing Granny to disappear.

As Mark leans in again, I see Granny start to open her mouth. I give her my sternest 'don't you dare' look, and for once, she seems to get the message. With a wink and a knowing smile, she fades away, leaving the two of us truly alone at last.

With Granny gone and the rest of the world fading into the background, I close my eyes and lean into the kiss, savoring this moment of peace and connection after all we've been through.

Also by Sloane Finley

Death by Dessert Series

Death by Chocolate Cupcake[1]

Death by Devil's Food Cake[2]

Ghostly Gumshoe Series

Granny's Ghost and the Haunted Homicide[3]

Granny's Ghost and the Poisoned Punch[4]

Granny's Ghost and the Bake-Off Bribe[5]

Granny's Ghost and the Deadly Dinner Party[6]

Granny's Ghost and the Movie Night Murder[7]

Granny's Ghost and the Murdered Medium[8]

Granny's Ghost and the Basement Burial[9]

Granny's Ghost and the Murdered Magician[10]

Granny's Ghost and the Deadly Delphinium[11]

Granny's Ghost and the Killer Caroler[12]

---

1. https://www.amazon.com/Death-Chocolate-Cupcake-Dessert-Mystery-ebook/dp/B0DPGS8S8Z
2. https://www.amazon.com/gp/product/B0DR7GTS38
3. https://www.amazon.com/gp/product/B0DFZR8LV6
4. https://www.amazon.com/gp/product/B0DGNN9QNK
5. https://www.amazon.com/gp/product/B0DHB1CBQL
6. https://www.amazon.com/gp/product/B0DJ7PW47X
7. https://www.amazon.com/gp/product/B0DJQ4R3L1
8. https://www.amazon.com/gp/product/B0DKB6Y47K
9. https://www.amazon.com/gp/product/B0DL3GRP97
10. https://www.amazon.com/gp/product/B0DLVJJJ33
11. https://www.amazon.com/gp/product/B0DMYJ5RQ6

Granny's Ghost and the Fatal Fashion Show[13]
Granny's Ghost and the Cook-Off Killer[14]
Ghostly Gumshoe Collection (Books 1 - 3)[15]

Fur-ensic Files Series
Fetch Me a Felon[16]
Best in Show, Worst in Murder[17]
Dachshund Dynasty[18]
Fur-ensic Files Complete Collection (Books 1 - 3)[19]

---

12. https://www.amazon.com/gp/product/B0DNY9H8YM
13. https://www.amazon.com/gp/product/B0DQHXXW7Z
14. https://www.amazon.com/gp/product/B0DRWFBDK4
15. https://www.amazon.com/Ghostly-Gumshoe-Collection-Paranormal-Mystery-ebook/dp/B0DHPDBYQ9
16. https://www.amazon.com/gp/product/B0DFVQMWV5
17. https://www.amazon.com/gp/product/B0DHPWBRFT
18. https://www.amazon.com/gp/product/B0DJG9KWYL
19. https://www.amazon.com/Fur-ensic-Files-Collection-Sloane-Finley-ebook/dp/B0DJZV9ZLZ

www.ingramcontent.com/pod-product-compliance
Ingram Content Group UK Ltd.
Pitfield, Milton Keynes, MK11 3LW, UK
UKHW021013180825
7441UKWH00015B/71